4 Irvine, R. R. (Robert R.)

The spoken word.

$17.95

DATE			

THE SPOKEN WORD

THE
SPOKEN
WORD

ROBERT IRVINE

St. Martin's Press

NEW YORK

To Ruth Cavin

Design by Glen M. Edelstein

Library of Congress Cataloging-in-Publication Data

Irvine, R. R. (Robert R.)
    The spoken word / Robert Irvine.
        p.   cm.
    "A Thomas Dunne book."
    ISBN 0-312-07841-2
    I. Title.
PS3559.R65S66   1992
813'.54—dc20   92-863
                                                CIP

First Edition: June 1992

10 9 8 7 6 5 4 3 2 1

Women may pray, testify, speak in tongues, and prophesy in the Church, when liberty is given by the Elders but not for the instruction of the Elders in their duties. Women may vote in the Church, and yet keep silence. It is their privilege to make and mend, and wash, and cook for the Saints, and lodge strangers, and wash the Saints' feet.

—Parley P. Pratt, Mormon Apostle murdered by the legal husband of his twelfth wife

Author's Note

The characters in this book are completely fictitious. Any resemblance to persons living or dead is purely coincidental. There is no position of First Apostle in the Church of Jesus Christ of Latter-day Saints, and the Danites are the product of legend.

1

The phone rang a second time as Moroni Traveler jerked awake. Two twenty-five A.M. glowed from the clock face. It was the dead of night. Only bad news came so late.

Heart pounding, he groped in the dark for the phone. His father, Martin, had gone out with a new lady friend last night, and Traveler hadn't heard him come home.

He pulled the receiver against his ear. "Yes."

"Is that you, Moroni?" The distraught voice belonged to his lifelong friend Willis Tanner.

Traveler swung his legs out of bed. Ice-cold linoleum shocked his feet. He should never have let his father go out in a rainstorm. "What's wrong, Willis?"

"I . . . I don't know how to say this."

Traveler stood on shaky knees.

"I don't like doing this, Moroni. I hope you understand that, but I don't have any choice."

The bedroom light snapped on. "For Christ's sake," Martin said from the doorway. "Who the hell's calling at this time of night?"

Traveler sagged back onto the bed. The breath he'd been holding leaked away.

"Well?" his father demanded.

"It's Willis, Dad."

"He ought to have more sense than to disturb an old man's rest at this time of night. Hang up on him."

Martin was still fully dressed.

"Don't hang up!" Tanner shouted.

Traveler yanked the phone away from his ear.

"The first time I laid eyes on that boy," Martin went on, "I knew he'd come to a bad end."

"Moroni!" Tanner hollered. "This is an emergency."

Martin said, "How many times have I told you? Never get involved with the church hierarchy, and that includes the likes of Willis Tanner."

Traveler held the phone out so his father could hear.

"Please," Tanner begged. "I need help."

"Hang up before it's too late," Martin said.

"Don't listen to him," Tanner cried. "Do you hear me, Mo?"

"There's no need to shout, Willis."

Martin pointed a finger at his son. "Whatever you do, don't get me involved in it."

"You owe me," Tanner said.

Shaking his head, Martin backed out of the bedroom and closed the door behind him.

Traveler sighed and brought the phone closer to his ear. He'd been waiting nearly a year for Willis to call in his debt.

"I have your promise on tape," Tanner reminded him. "You said you'd do anything as long as I helped you."

"Quit while you're ahead," Traveler replied. "Just tell me what you want at this time of night."

"Meet me at the temple."

"Inside?"

"More or less."

The back of Traveler's neck prickled. Salt Lake City's Mormon Temple was strictly out of bounds to the likes of him, a nonbeliever, a Gentile. Crossing its threshold would be sacrilege.

"Why aren't we using your office?" Traveler asked.

"I'll have someone waiting for you at the south gate."

"It's raining, for God's sake."

"Not anymore."

Traveler listened. Gone was the week-long sound of rain pounding the roof.

"We don't have time to waste," Tanner said and hung up.

The dashboard clock read 3:05. It had been reading that since the Ford Fairmont's warranty ran out. It was correct twice a day, now being one of them.

Traveler stared into the darkness. To be sure, the rain was gone. What Willis hadn't said was that it had turned to snow.

April showers bring May flowers, Traveler reminded himself as he pulled out of the driveway and headed down First Avenue. Only this particular April downfall was so heavy the Fairmont's headlights couldn't penetrate more than a few yards. For good measure, there were no tire tracks in the foot-deep, overnight accumulation.

He blazed a trail to the corner and turned onto South Temple Street, hoping the main thoroughfare might have been cleared. All he found was a few deep ruts. He drove them as best he could.

Windshield mist, fed by the defroster, forced him to drive one-handed while wiping the glass with the other. He kept his speed to fifteen miles an hour, the car fishtailing constantly. Martin had been after him for weeks to buy new tires with proper treads.

Leaning forward, Traveler squinted through his misty peephole. A yellow glow brought his foot off the accelerator. Instantly, the Ford began sliding sideways. The glow turned red. Traveler eased back onto the accelerator, intending to run the traffic signal.

Movement glimpsed out of the corner of his eye triggered his reflexes. He jerked the steering wheel away from the oncoming snowplow.

The sedan spun in a full circle before skidding to a stop across both traffic lanes. The engine died. Traveler braced himself for an impact. All he got was a continuous blast from an air-horn as the plow driver swung around the Fairmont and continued down South Temple. The sound persisted long after the plow had passed by.

Traveler restarted the engine, maneuvered the Ford back onto course, and followed in the plow's wake. Its curved blade, only wide enough to clear a single lane, was funneling a continuous snowbank three feet high along the curb.

Traveler fell back as far as he could without losing sight of the plow in the storm. When the defroster threatened to make that impossible, he rolled down his window to let in the cold. The windshield cleared. He took a deep breath. Somehow, the snow smelled cleaner than the rain that had been falling for so long.

At Fifth East, another signal turned red. Logic told him to keep on going. But instinct got the better of him again. He tapped the brake pedal. The Ford made a beeline for the curb, burying itself in the freshly created snowbank.

Traveler immediately rocked the car, shifting gears back and forth from forward to reverse. After a few seconds, the Ford's transmission shuddered like a dying animal. He put it out of its misery by switching off the engine.

"Thank you, Willis Tanner."

The temple was still a good mile away. The wind-chill factor, according to the radio, was ten degrees below freezing.

With a groan Traveler climbed out of the car and started down South Temple Street, keeping to the cleared traffic lane. At State Street, the plow had turned left, leaving Traveler two blocks of trailblazing. Ice balls quickly formed on his jeans; snow began working its way into his galoshes. His feet, sensing the onslaught of frostbite, started to itch.

With each struggling step Traveler remembered his father's parting remarks. "Willis has no right to call you out in weather like this."

"I owe him," Traveler had answered. "You know that."

"I warned you, Moroni. You should never have asked for his help."

"There was no other way."

"It didn't change anything. Claire's still dead."

"The debt has to be paid," Traveler said. "The sooner the better."

Martin helped Traveler into his fleece-lined coat. "It's women, Mo. You and I don't have any luck with them."

"Don't start."

"They give us trouble but still we can't forget them. Their memory stays with us like static cling."

"I don't see you giving them up," Traveler said.

"You're talking about my new lady friend, aren't you? Jolene's a fine-looking woman. You'll have to admit that." Martin grinned. "If I'd known you were going out tonight, I'd have stayed over at her place instead of coming home to keep you company."

"Anytime you want to bring a woman home I'll make sure you have plenty of privacy."

"You've got to be careful where you take a woman. Bring them home and they start thinking about marriage."

"I can always move out and find myself an apartment," Traveler said.

"Who'd keep an eye on you then?"

"I'll tell you what. I can drop you off at Jolene's on the way downtown."

"Have you ever had a woman put her cold feet on you in the middle of the night? Something like that could give a man my age a heart attack. No, sir. On a night like this, stay away from women with cold feet."

Martin had put a hand on Traveler's arm. "Willis Tanner's no better, you know. He's a cold man when it comes to Gentiles like us."

2

Willis Tanner was pacing back and forth in front of the South Temple gate. He'd been there long enough for snow to accumulate on the shoulders of his camel's hair overcoat. At Traveler's approach, he brushed nervously at the flakes as if ridding himself of unsightly dandruff.

"What kept you? I've been going crazy," Tanner said in a rush.

His outburst brought two men out from behind the temple wall. They looked like what they were, church security, probably ex-FBI, big men with unbuttoned overcoats in case they had to get to their weapons. They dwarfed Tanner, though Traveler had some pounds on them.

"I told you it was an emergency," Tanner said. "Why did you waste time walking here?"

"Your technique's showing, Willis. I refuse to feel guilty because my car's stuck in a snowbank."

Tanner ducked his head, avoiding eye contact. His hat brim dumped snow at Traveler's feet.

"I've walked damn near a mile," Traveler told him. "My feet are half frozen and water's dripping down the back of my neck."

Instead of responding, Tanner turned and entered the temple grounds. Until then, Traveler hadn't noticed the briefcase chained to his friend's wrist.

Traveler stepped carefully, following in Tanner's booted footprints. Behind them, the temple gate clanked shut. After a moment, the security men caught up with Traveler, breaking their own trail in order to flank him like a military escort.

Directly ahead, ground lights glowed in the falling snow, illuminating the temple's iron inner fence, the boundary beyond which only the faithful could pass. It was still too dark to see the temple itself, though Traveler sensed its massive presence.

Tanner veered to the right, away from the temple fence and toward a squat gray granite building that wasn't much larger than a family mausoleum. There, he paused to knock on a bronze door covered with sea gulls in bas-relief. The birds, shown in flight, were carved with yawning, hungry beaks. That hunger had saved the Mormon pioneers from a plague of locusts and gave the birds a permanent place in church symbology.

The door opened with quiet, vaultlike precision. Bright light spilled out, glaring off the snow. One of Traveler's escorts touched him on the shoulder. He took the hint and followed Tanner into a small antechamber, where another pair of security men were waiting. The granite alcove was bare and windowless. Traveler found himself facing a second bronze door, which showed beehives instead of sea gulls.

"I'm sorry," Tanner said, "but you'll have to be searched." He held up his hand to forestall argument. When Traveler said nothing, Tanner began rubbing his left eye, the one that tended to squint when he was nervous. "That is the spoken word of the prophet."

"I should have listened to my father. Never mix business and religion."

"I can't break the rules, not even for a friend. When the prophet speaks . . ." Tanner shrugged.

"All right, Willis." Traveler took off his coat, tossed it to a security man, and raised his hands. "Just tell me when we're even and the debt's paid off."

The body search was personal enough to make Traveler clench his teeth.

"Don't look at me like that, Mo." Tanner unchained himself from the briefcase, then handed his camel's hair coat to one security man. The other guard opened the inner door with his card. A granite-lined tunnel sloped down into the earth.

"We'll go on alone," Tanner told the security men. He reattached the case before leading the way.

Lights had been set into the walls at close intervals, coinciding with areas of blackened stone, apparently where torches had lit the tunnel before the advent of electricity. Somewhere, machinery throbbed. Unseen vents flooded the tunnel with warm air.

After a while, the slope gave way to stone steps. By then, Traveler guessed they must have been deep underground. The granite walls felt cold and clammy.

Tanner stopped in front of another bronze door. This one was guarded by a remote television camera perched on a rock ledge above the lintel.

"Where the hell are we?" Traveler asked.

"You're treading new ground, Moroni, where no Gentile has gone before. Phone men, plumbers, electricians, even the cleaning crew must have temple recommends to enter this, God's kingdom."

"I'm beginning to understand how the fatted calf felt."

Tanner turned his gaze from Traveler to the camera lens. The door opened almost immediately.

"Welcome to the temple's security center," Tanner said as soon as they were inside.

The room, a good forty feet square, was crammed with computers, phone gear, and dozens of TV monitors, plus the technicians to go with them. A few of the TV screens were dark; others carried exterior shots of the temple gates and grounds, the tabernacle, and several vast rooms that Traveler suspected to be interior shots of the temple itself.

"What do you think?" Tanner asked.

"Meeting in your office would have been a hell of a lot easier."

"This area is absolutely secure."

"You're making me nervous, Willis."

"Come on. We'll use the conference room."

Traveler followed Tanner through another door. Beyond it was another forty-foot room. Only this one contained nothing but a massive oak table, surrounded by chairs. Traveler counted them, twelve matching chairs upholstered in maroon velvet, and one larger chair done in gold fabric. He took a deep breath. He was looking at seating for the Twelve Apostles and the Prophet.

The walls were like windows into Mormon scripture. Floor-to-ceiling murals depicted the Angel Moroni delivering the golden tablets to Joseph Smith on the Hill Cumorah, Smith's martyrdom at the hands of Illinois Masons, and Brigham Young's trek to the promised land.

Tanner pointed at the ceiling, where Renaissance angels were at work building the temple.

"No, you don't, Willis. Men did the dirty work. They always do. What kind of dirty work do you want from me?"

Traveler headed for the golden chair slowly enough to allow Tanner to intercept and steer him into one of the others.

"I know you, Mo," Tanner said. "At heart you're a Saint."

Traveler turned away to study his namesake on the wall. The Angel Moroni's foreshortened finger was pointing at him like a wartime recruiting poster. *Join the Church of Jesus Christ of Latter-day Saints and see the world.*

"Stop playing missionary, Willis. I'm cold, wet, and tired."

Tanner unchained the briefcase and laid it on the table. "Shortly before you arrived, Moroni, I spoke to the prophet, may God protect him."

"I hope he's well."

"Dear God," Tanner said. "You've heard the rumors, haven't you?"

"Willis, you called me here. I didn't volunteer."

Tanner sucked a quick breath. "You understand, there hasn't been any mention of this in the media. As far as you're concerned, as far as anyone is, Elton Woolley is on retreat, praying for guidance, and has been for the past several months. That's what you've heard, isn't it?"

"I'll be damned," Traveler said. Until that moment, he'd completely dismissed the stories being spread by his friend Mad Bill. "He's ill, isn't he?"

Tanner rubbed his drooping left eyelid. "Tell me you didn't hear it from the Sandwich Prophet, please."

"I'm afraid I did."

"Dear God, not on one of his sandwich boards?"

"Bill hasn't gone that far yet."

"What then?" Tanner said, squinting.

"I wasn't really paying attention."

"I've got to know the worst."

"Come on, Willis. You know Bill. He's always spreading his prophecies, one way or another."

Tanner held a hand over his face.

"All Bill told me was that the prophet's illness is proof that the devil has risen, that the end of the Mormon Church is at hand." Traveler shrugged. "I put it down to wishful thinking on his part."

"There's more to it than that. I can see it on your face."

"That's everything, Willis. You have my word on it."

Tanner blinked away his squint. "I've said it before, I'll say it again. The prophet thinks of you as a fallen angel."

"Don't start, Willis. Tell me what you want without the sales pitch."

"You are the Angel Moroni's namesake."

Traveler sighed; he'd heard it all before. "I was named for my father."

"Calling himself Martin because he doesn't like Moroni changes nothing."

"Thank you, Willis. I'll put that in the Yellow Pages. Moroni Traveler and Son, Angelic Detectives."

"The prophet asked for you by name. 'Only my fallen angel

will do,' he said. Those were his exact words. Few men are so honored."

"Do you know what my father said before I left home? 'Go back on your word if you have to, but don't get involved with Willis Tanner or his church.'"

Tanner bowed his head and clasped his hands together. "The prophet is failing, Moroni. He has been for some time. What's happened now could kill him."

"What do you want from me?"

"As I told you on the phone, I'm calling in my marker. As of now you belong to us, for the duration."

Traveler stared. There was something in Tanner's face Traveler had never seen before. A fearful hollowness to his eyes, as if the certainty of his beliefs had suddenly deserted him.

Tanner unlocked the briefcase and extracted a small, buff-colored envelope, which he handed to Traveler.

The envelope was addressed to Traveler personally. The prophet's shaky hand was immediately recognizable. The notepaper matched the envelope. At the top of the page, the initials EW appeared in gold. There was no date.

Dear Moroni,

My grandniece, Lael, has been kidnapped. Because of the circumstances, I've prayed for guidance. I've searched my soul seeking the proper course of action. Only one answer has come to me. It will take an investigator named for an angel to prevail against the forces of evil. I beg your help achieving God's will.

Your servant,
Elton Woolley

3

Traveler found himself standing in front of the Hill Cumorah. The blinding golden light surrounding the Angel Moroni seemed to radiate its own heat. Only when Traveler reached out to warm his hands did he notice that furnace vents had been integrated into the mural.

He turned his back on the deception and stared at Willis Tanner.

"You understood the consequences when you asked me for a favor," Tanner said. "You knew I'd want repayment one day."

Traveler lurched forward, intending to use his size to intimidate Tanner as he'd done so many times before. But his friend didn't budge from his chair. He merely held out his hand and snapped his fingers. "The note, Moroni. I want it back."

Traveler slipped the paper into its envelope before returning it. Tanner immediately set fire to it. An instant before the flames reached his fingers, he dropped the charred remains into a metal wastebasket at his feet.

"I appreciate the prophet's faith in me," Traveler said, "and the debt I owe, but kidnapping belongs to the FBI."

"God reveals Himself through our prophets. Who are we to question Him?" Tanner's untroubled, certain-of-salvation look had returned.

Traveler sat down again and closed his eyes. Under normal circumstances, sticking his nose into a kidnapping could cost him his investigator's license. Or worse, if the FBI really got pissed. Utah, however, was different. Here, Elton Woolley always had the last word.

"Believe in Him," Tanner said. Whether he referred to the prophet or to God was unclear.

Traveler launched himself out of the chair and headed back over to the Angel Moroni on the Hill Cumorah. Up close, the painted image disappeared into brush stroke and technique.

"Talk to me," Tanner said.

Traveler turned his back on the angel. "A man like Elton Woolley is guarded more closely than the president. So tell me something. How would kidnappers be able to get in touch with him?"

"They phoned."

"Come on, Willis. You don't expect me to believe that God's living prophet on earth answers his own phone?"

"The number's unlisted, of course. It doesn't even show up in the reverse telephone directories."

"What does that tell you?"

"They didn't actually reach him."

"Who then?"

"The First Apostle, Elihu Moseby. Moseby's assistant, my counterpart, had just stepped out. It was a fluke."

Traveler moved back to the table and sat down. "All right. Tell me about it."

"Everything I say here is strictly confidential. You understand that, don't you?" Tanner waited for Traveler's nod before continuing. "During Elton Woolley's illness, the First Apostle has temporarily assumed the prophet's duties. That includes working out of the prophet's office in the Hotel Utah."

"They must have gotten the phone number from the missing girl."

Tanner leaned forward and whispered, "Keep your voice down."

"In case you've forgotten, Willis, we're in a sealed room under the temple. Now tell me, how many people know about the call?"

"Only the inner circle."

"Are you talking apostles, or what?"

"Not all twelve. Not as yet."

"Who else?" Traveler said.

"No one."

"Moseby's assistant?"

"No one."

"Did you record the call?"

"That's procedure. Moseby delivered my copy personally so no one else would be involved."

"I'd like to hear it."

"I know it by heart," Tanner said. " 'We have your grand-niece, Lael Woolley. You have one week before she dies.' " He took a deep breath. "They thought they were talking to the prophet."

"One week from today."

"From yesterday. The call came in late last night. Moseby insisted on consulting the prophet before taking any kind of action."

"Dammit, Willis. You can't expect one man to do this kind of job."

"Watch your language, especially here." Tanner looked up expectantly. "You were chosen because we can't bring in the police. Or the FBI. If too many people know about the kidnapping, it's certain to get out. Besides, you read the prophet's note. Only a man named Moroni can prevail."

"Your tic's back, Willis."

Tanner ignored him.

"What are you keeping back?" Traveler said. "The ransom, I take it."

"The prophet can't be seen as vulnerable." Tanner rubbed

his eyes. "Not now, not when he's so ill. Remember that when you're looking for the girl."

"I haven't agreed yet."

"I know you, Moroni. You won't walk out as long as you owe me one."

"Let's get back to the call. With all the security equipment you've got, you must know where it came from."

"A pay phone over on Second East, near Lou's Wagon Lunch. I can get you the number if you want."

Traveler waved away the offer. "My advice to you, strictly as an outsider, you understand, is to negotiate with these people. Buy yourself some time, so your security service can go to work."

"Why should they call again? All they have to do is wait for their headlines."

"Now we're getting to it. What headlines?"

"There are vile rumors sweeping the land, Moroni."

"I know, the devil has risen. We've already been through that."

"It's being spray-painted all over town." Tanner tucked his hands into his armpits.

Traveler leaned forward until only inches separated them. "I want everything, Willis. Otherwise, I take Martin's advice and renege on my debt."

"Should you ever repeat what I'm about to say outside these walls, I'll deny it. Even under oath."

Traveler backed off, giving his friend breathing room.

"As you know," Tanner said, taking a deep breath, "God reveals Himself to our prophets as He did in the beginning with Joseph Smith."

He extracted his hands and blew on them. His fingers looked as white as his face. His teeth chattered. The sound seemed to drive away his tic.

The last time Traveler had seen Tanner in such a state was the day the bishop caught them smoking behind the ward house.

When Tanner continued, speaking through clenched teeth,

each word sounded painful. "The kidnappers have demanded a false revelation, one that would give women equal rights within the church. They want female membership in the priesthood. Lael will be released only when such a revelation is made public in the newspapers. If it isn't printed, she dies."

"My God," Traveler said, coming out of his chair. "It's about time you people joined the twentieth century."

Tanner shook his head. "There's no leeway here. We follow God's spoken word."

"All you have to do is give women equal rights and the ransom's moot."

"God will not be coerced," Tanner said.

"Neither will I, Willis." Traveler moved away from his friend and began pacing alongside Brigham Young's wagon train.

"The prophet trusts you, Moroni."

Traveler paused to stare Brigham in the eye. "You can't keep something like this a secret. Sooner or later word gets out. Then what?"

"God won't let us down."

"No you don't. If something goes wrong, I'm going to be the one who gets the blame."

"The prophet—"

"Use your own security people," Traveler interrupted. He turned his back on Brigham Young and walked over to a group of women pulling handcarts. His great-grandmother had made such a trip, hauling a load from Council Bluffs to Salt Lake across the Great Plains and the Rocky Mountains.

"You can't expect me to handle something like this," Traveler said.

Tanner dipped into the briefcase again. This time he came up with an audiocassette. "When I helped you find Claire's killer, you said you'd do anything I asked in return. Would you like to hear your exact words?"

"Considering the situation, I want to speak to the prophet personally."

"The doctors say it's touch and go at the moment."

"If he dies, the kidnappers lose their leverage," Traveler said.

"Until then, Mo, you belong to him."

"What happens if I say no."

"This is our land, Mo. The promised land. No one finds work here if the church says otherwise."

Traveler returned to his maroon chair. "I've known you damn near all my life, Willis. When the bishop caught us, those were your cigarettes. When your mother smelled liquor on us, you were the one with the bottle."

"What's your point?"

"If the shit hits the fan, Willis, you're not coming out smelling like a rose this time."

Tanner shrugged. "At the prophet's suggestion, I've prepared a sealed file on his niece. She's his grandniece, really, but he usually calls her his niece." An envelope came out of his briefcase.

"Am I allowed to take this with me?" Traveler said.

"As long as you treat it as confidential."

"I want to hear what you know about the girl."

"Lael Woolley's not exactly a girl. She's twenty, twenty-one next month. She was a theology student at Brigham Young University until recently when she dropped out to become active in the feminist movement."

"Jesus, Willis."

"Please, Moroni, no blasphemy. Not here." Tanner stared at the ceiling as if expecting lightning bolts.

"Have you considered the possibility that there is no kidnapping, that the girl and her feminists might be up to something?"

"If you knew Lael, you'd realize that's impossible."

"I don't know *you* that well."

Tanner smiled; the lip movement set off his tic. "She joined a women's group calling itself the Army of Nauvoo. So far, they've done nothing more aggressive than peddling pamphlets and sending out recruiters."

Traveler caught himself before he could swear again. He

swallowed the urge but couldn't contain a snort of approval at the name chosen by the women. Nauvoo, Illinois, was where Joseph Smith announced his revelation making polygamy a tenet of the Mormon Church.

"I'll need a list of her friends," Traveler said.

Tanner nodded. "She's an unusual girl, but then you'll find that out for yourself soon enough. She doesn't have many close friends her age, not even in school. The names I came up with are mostly women in the Army of Nauvoo."

He broke the seal on the manila envelope containing the file and read the names. "Amanda Ware and Jemma Hoyt. They're both officers in the group."

"What about boyfriends?" Traveler asked.

"She's not that unusual. His name is Dwight Hafen. He's a part-time instructor at BYU, working on his doctorate in LDS history. Most days you'll find him doing research at the church library."

"Have you talked to him?"

"Just on the phone. I kept it casual. I didn't say she was missing, or anything like that. He claims that he and Lael broke up a while back, though that's news to the prophet. Hafen says they had a fight about the company she was keeping. I can't blame him, considering the lesbians who hang around these feminist groups."

"Is that Hafen speaking or you?"

"Finding out things like that is your specialty. He'll be waiting for you at the church library as soon as it's light."

"I'll set my own schedule," Traveler said.

"Whatever you want, but Hafen will be on standby until you say otherwise. I've already seen to that."

Traveler took a moment to glance at the file. The church's computers had been hard at work, compiling printouts of Lael's classes at BYU, including the names of instructors and all fellow students. Additional teacher/student lists went back to her first-grade class at Wasatch School. Her home address was followed by a printout of all neighbors in a two-block area. The biography page listed Lael's father as Seth Woolley, the son of the prophet's dead brother, David; her mother's name was Ida. Half a photograph had been clipped to the top of the first page.

Traveler held it up.

"I had to edit it for security purposes," Tanner said. "She was standing next to the prophet."

Traveler blinked. A trick of light, a faulty camera setting, unexpected movement, a film flaw, just about anything could account for he was seeing. "Is this a good likeness?"

"I knew she'd interest you," Tanner said.

The young woman staring at Traveler was extremely thin and fragile looking. Her obligatory smile into the camera made a sharp contrast to her sad, brooding eyes. Her hair was parted in the middle and pulled straight back, perhaps into a ponytail, though that didn't show. He had the feeling that Lael Woolley had tried to make herself look unattractive and old-fashioned deliberately. She hadn't succeeded.

"I saw it too," Tanner said. "She reminds you of Claire, doesn't she?"

"They're nothing alike," Traveler said, shaking his head. But Tanner was right. Something about Lael brought back memories of Claire.

"The girl's very close to the prophet, you understand. He never had children of his own, and his only nephew had just the one, Lael. In any case, she's been living at home with her mother since leaving BYU. Her parents, I'm sorry to say, are divorced."

"Tell me about the Army of Nauvoo," Traveler said.

"They started out harmlessly enough, a group of church-going ladies banding together to help the less fortunate. But somewhere along the line they strayed from the word and began demanding membership into our priesthood."

"Just like the ransom note," Traveler observed.

"For the moment these women are still church members, but we have to conclude that their recent conduct makes them suspect. Only last month they picketed our offices and demanded a meeting with the prophet, though that was out of the question. God knows why Lael would join such a group."

"Now that you mention it, I remember reading about the picketers in the paper."

Tanner clicked his tongue. "We've done our best to keep a lid on their coverage. Nothing in the *Deseret News,* of course, though the *Tribune* has let us down on occasion."

"That's because you don't own the *Trib.*"

"Lately, we've heard that the Army of Nauvoo has affiliated itself with the Sisters Cumorah."

"I've never heard of them."

"They're new and more radical, and have gone so far as to leave fliers at the temple gates. They've declared war on men. They—" Tanner glanced at the mural of Joseph Smith receiving enlightenment from the Angel Moroni "—they say hostilities began when Joe Smith's testosterone got the better of him and he opted for polygamy. Understand, this isn't me speaking, but it's part of my job to keep informed, to protect the prophet in any way necessary. In any case, the Sisters Cumorah claim that the church hasn't been safe for women since Smith's revelation. It's blasphemy, of course, but I wanted you to know the kind of people you're up against."

Traveler studied the photograph again. "I can't see any of Elton Woolley's kin, niece or grandniece, joining such a group."

"As far as church policy is concerned, there's no difference between the two organizations. They both do the work of the devil, though no one's been excommunicated as yet."

"Are you saying that Lael Woolley has joined the devil?"

Tanner sighed. "I'm just telling you the situation, that's all."

"Why is it I'm not reassured?"

"You would be if you had faith."

"If I'm going to work on this, I'll need a contract," Traveler said. "Signed by the prophet."

"I've arranged to have you paid at your regular rate, though technically speaking this is a favor you're returning. The work should be done for nothing."

"My father will need a contract, too, because I'm going to need him on this."

Tanner nodded. "The prophet told me it might be best to use both Moronis."

"Put it in writing, Willis."

"I'll do better than that."

With great care, Tanner unzipped a document compartment inside his briefcase. He withdrew a business-size envelope, which he gave to Traveler. The flap wasn't sealed. The letter inside was typewritten on church letterhead.

To whom it may concern:
The bearer of this letter, Mr. Moroni Traveler, is on official business for the Church of Jesus Christ of Latter-day Saints. Any assistance given to him will be considered an act of faith and be suitably rewarded.

Alma 9:28. "Therefore, prepare ye the way of the Lord, for the time is at hand that all men shall reap a reward of their works, according to that which they have been—if they have been righteous they shall reap the salvation of their souls, according to the power and deliverance of Jesus Christ."

Should monetary compensation be necessary, the Church of Jesus Christ of Latter-day Saints hereby promises to back Mr. Traveler to the full extent of its resources.

Elton Woolley

"It's better than a contract," Tanner said. "It's practically a carte blanche."

"You win, Willis. I'm impressed."

"We've set up a twenty-four-hour command center with a special phone number. Someone in authority will always be available to you."

Traveler took a deep breath.

"Well?" Tanner said. "What do you say?"

"I can't go to work until you show me how to get out of this underground maze."

4

Traveler emerged into a balmy dawn. The temperature had jumped a good thirty degrees. A downpour of warm rain was quickly turning last night's snow into a watery slush.

As soon as the temple gates closed behind him, Traveler lowered his head and waded across the overflowing street toward his office. When he glanced up at the top floor of the Chester Building, he saw a light in the window of Moroni Traveler and Son. Perhaps Martin's curiosity had gotten the better of him; perhaps he'd come in early to hear the results of Willis Tanner's call for help.

Traveler shook his head. More likely one or the other of them had forgotten to turn out the light last night. In which case, the building's owner and namesake, Barney Chester, would remind them of their transgression soon enough.

Traveler bypassed the bronze revolving door, an art deco survivor like the rest of the building, and fitted his key into an adjoining plate-glass portal. What dim light was visible in the lobby came from the cigar stand's perpetual flame.

A kind of wet-dog smell, pungent but not exactly unpleasant, announced the residency of Mad Bill and his Navajo disciple, Charlie Redwine. The pair, along with their recent convert, Newel Ellsworth, had permission to shelter in the Chester Building during bad weather. To keep most of the tenants happy, they had to clear away their bedding and vacate the premises during business hours.

Traveler, blinking water from his eyes, headed for the stairs since it was was too early for the elevator to be running. He was tiptoeing past the cigar stand when Charlie rose up from behind the display counter.

"Sorry," Traveler whispered. "I didn't mean to wake you."

"A shaman never sleeps, not when the dark spirits are restless."

Since the Indian was fully dressed, Traveler almost believed him.

"What the hell's going on?" Bill asked without showing himself.

Charlie Redwine tucked his peyote bag necklace inside his checkered shirt, then folded his arms over his chest. It was one of his movie Indian poses, a declaration that he intended to remain mute. He'd speak again only when his arms relaxed.

"Business hours don't start till eight," Bill complained.

"I thought the Church of the True Prophet never closed," Traveler said.

Yawning, Bill revealed himself. He was wearing a gray sweatshirt decorated with a blue CTP logo. His homespun prophet's robe hung tentlike over his sandwich board, which was leaning against the magazine rack.

Charlie loosened his arms long enough to rattle the coffee can that Bill called their "poor box."

Traveler dropped a ten among the salted coins.

"Manna from heaven," Bill said. "Your sandwich prophet thanks you."

The lobby lights came on. Traveler turned to see Newel Ellsworth standing in front of the restroom door with his hand on the wall switch.

"I heard voices," he said.

The lights revealed two sleeping bags laid out side by side near the end of the cigar counter.

When Ellsworth saw Traveler glance at the bedding, he jerked a thumb over his shoulder. "I sleep close to the toilets, because of my weak bladder."

Bill craned his head to check the regulator clock. "Moroni didn't come here at five in the morning to discuss our sleeping arrangements."

Charlie snorted. His arms unfolded. "I sensed his coming."

"That's because the poor box was empty," Bill said.

Ellsworth stared at the coffee can and wet his lips.

Bill said, "You must pray, Newel. You must steel yourself until the liquor stores open."

The man sighed so hard his chest collapsed. Until conversion, he'd led a nomadic existence as a West Temple wino. Now he was the number-three man in the Church of the True Prophet, behind Bill and his apostle, Charlie.

Like Charlie, Ellsworth must have slept in his clothes. Now that Traveler thought about it, he'd never seen Ellsworth without his hunter's jacket, a khaki-colored garment several sizes too big for him. Its maze of cartridge pouches and pockets bulged with what the man said were his worldly possessions. Beneath the jacket he wore a vest with yet more pockets. In these he kept pencils, pens, and three-by-five cards on which he constantly made notes.

A wine-ruined face made his age impossible to pinpoint, though Traveler figured it somewhere around fifty. Too young for the World War II exploits he often bragged about.

"So tell us, Moroni," Bill said. "Why are you here this early?"

"I can't discuss it."

Bill shook his head. "I saw you, Moroni. I was watching from your office a while ago."

"You left the lights on."

"Charlie and I were standing there contemplating the glory of God's universe when you entered the temple gate across the street."

"What were you smoking?"

24

"Peyote is part of our religion, you know that."

Traveler glanced at the puddle gathering around his feet. "I'm going upstairs to change my clothes."

"You're not getting away that easily." Bill grabbed his robe and swept it from the sandwich board, revealing the day's gospel: Satan Has Risen.

Traveler groaned inwardly. Were fresh rumors spreading already? Had Tanner's security precautions failed? He nodded at the sign. "What's your point with this one?"

"My point!" Bill thumped himself on the chest. "You're the one who should be explaining, a Gentile treading on holy ground."

"Just tell me the truth. It's important."

"There have been people coming and going across the street all night, but only one Gentile that I recognized." Bill pulled the robe over his head and cinched it at the waist. "Had there been no guards, I would have seen fit to stand at your side, Moroni, in the flesh instead of spirit only."

Traveler nudged the sandwich board with his toe. "This could get you into trouble. You and Charlie both."

"I won't be censored by the church." Bill nodded at Ellsworth, who dug into his vest for a pencil and a blank card. "I've named Newel as my chronicler. He's going to turn my life into a book. A saga like David and Goliath, with me taking on the church."

Traveler sighed. Only yesterday, Ellsworth had claimed to be an undercover reporter investigating the plight of Salt Lake's homeless.

Traveler stepped behind the counter, where Barney kept a hot plate and coffee pot. As always, the pot had been filled the night before. All Traveler had to do was switch on the power.

"Tell me about the poster," he said, warning his hands near the electric coils. "Tell me about Satan."

Bill hesitated, glancing at Ellsworth.

"I understand," Ellsworth said. "I'm not yet a member of the inner council." He pocketed his pencil and paper and ambled into the men's room.

Bill took a deep breath. "This is different. I admit it. I've done just about everything with my boards, soliciting funds, advertising myself, you name it. But not this time. This time, it's truly God's work."

Charlie's hand slipped inside his shirt as if to scratch himself. But Traveler knew that the Navajo was working his peyote bag.

"The word is out, Moroni. All you have to do is listen. All you have to do is read the writing on the walls. It's more than graffiti. It's . . ." Bill gestured helplessly.

"I've seen Charlie spraying on your messages in the past."

"You're absolutely right, Mo. It's not kids this time. It's street people who've taken up the cause."

"Whose cause are we talking about?"

"Yours. Everybody's. Mine, too. Mormons and Gentiles alike, with Charlie and I proselytizing among them all. We spread the word as we have been for years." Bill shook his head. "Only now are people listening."

From the men's room came the sound of a toilet being flushed, then another.

"The spirits are making Newel restless," Charlie said.

Bill looked up. Traveler followed his gaze to the massive marble columns that flanked the cigar stand. The columns ended in Doric capitals abutting on a ceiling on which a WPA mural depicted the 1847 pioneer trek into Salt Lake.

Bill said, "The old stories are coming back, Moroni. Tales I haven't heard since I was a boy. Ones my grandfather used to tell me, between times when he was reading the scriptures out for the whole family to hear. About the coming battle between good and evil."

Traveler squinted at the painting of Brigham Young and his wagon train. The painting, unlike the mural in the temple basement, was more dramatic than spiritual. Barney Chester claimed it was the work of Thomas Hart Benton.

"My people have heard the stories too," Charlie said, "from their shamans."

Bill's gaze came back to earth. "I don't like it."

"You've been predicting catastrophe for years with your sandwich boards," Traveler said, hoping that Bill's demons had nothing to do with Willis Tanner's. "If they're coming true, you should be happy."

"That was business, Mo. This . . ." Bill's shoulders rose and fell. "Something is wrong in the promised land. Something beyond faith. It's as if Satan is really among us, walking the land in search of those he can drag down to hell. We must be on guard constantly. If he whispers promises in our ears, we must be deaf."

Traveler felt somewhat shaken because there was usually a grain of truth in Mad Bill's meanderings. He reached out and grasped his friend's arm. "I need to know details."

"Like what, Moroni?" Bill leaned forward and stared into Traveler's eyes. After several seconds of silence, he nodded. "You're serious, aren't you? You believe."

"Tell me what to believe in."

Bill busied himself pouring coffee for the three of them. He added canned milk and sugar to his cup and sipped slowly, not speaking until finally Traveler nudged him. "Twice I've been told this story. It's about a Mormon prophet who broke the church's covenant with God. A prophet who usurped God's will. Who used God's revelation for his own purposes and thereby became Satan's creature."

"Which prophet?" Traveler asked.

"As I said, it's a recurring story. Like the old wives' tales about Brigham Young murdering Joe Smith to take control of the church. They both go back to my childhood. I can't remember how many Mormon prophets ago that was."

Traveler turned to the Indian. "What about you, Charlie? Have you or your spirits heard anything specific?"

"The Lamanite time of power is at hand."

In Mormon scripture, Indians were known as Lamanites, the lost tribe of Israel. As such, Navajos like Charlie were prime targets for LDS missionaries.

Traveler strode across the lobby to the front window. Outside, it was raining harder than ever. The snow had disappeared completely, leaving a street-wide river in its wake. When he turned to retrace his steps, Bill and Charlie were right behind him.

"I want to hire you for the next few days," he told them. "All three of you."

The pair exchanged wary looks before Charlie trotted back to the men's room and rapped on the door. Ellsworth appeared so quickly he must have been waiting on the other side.

"We've got a job," Charlie said loud enough to echo.

"How much does it pay?"

Traveler smiled. Willis Tanner was in no position to balk at expenses. Besides, hiring the trio would give Traveler a way of keeping them in eating money during the storm without having to resort to charity.

"I'm paying five dollars an hour," Traveler said as soon as they'd gathered around. "Apiece."

Ellsworth took out a pencil and held it poised over one of his three-by-five cards.

"I want you out on the streets, listening for me," Traveler said. "I want to know every rumor you hear. I don't care if it's about God, Satan, or secret wives. If it has anything to do with the church, report it to me."

5

Moroni Traveler and Son was a single corner room on the top floor of the Chester Building. One window faced east toward the Wasatch Mountains, the other looked out on the temple. At the moment, falling rain was the only thing visible.

Traveler tossed his wet clothes onto his desk, which faced his father's. Both desks were old-fashioned teacher's models of polished oak with sunken typewriter wells. Martin had bought them as surplus when the school district switched to Formica.

Traveler dried himself and changed into the spare set of clothes he kept at the office. When he phoned for a cab, the dispatcher advised him that walking was not only better exercise but quicker, since the company's garage was under water.

For a moment, he considered calling his father. But the last thing he wanted was to get Martin out in this kind of weather.

Annoyed with himself for not borrowing Martin's rugged Jeep Cherokee in first place, Traveler checked the Yellow Pages. The nearest car rental was a mile down West Temple Street. He called and got a recording telling him to wait his turn. When it came, he reserved the only four-wheel-drive vehicle available, a full-size pickup truck.

By the time he left his office the elevator was running. As always Nephi Bates was at the helm, armed with his *Book of Mormon* and a cassette player loaded with the Tabernacle Choir. His pinched face grew a smile at the sight of Traveler.

"I'm surprised to find you working on the Sabbath," Traveler said.

"The faithful await you," Bates responded.

Traveler hesitated in front of the grillwork cage.

"On the second floor," Bates clarified. "I let them use the vacant office. Old Doctor Rigdon's place."

"Who are they?"

"They didn't give names."

"What's this about the faithful?" Traveler said.

Bates ducked his head, but not before Traveler caught a glimpse of avarice in his eyes. Whoever was waiting on the second floor had probably paid for the privilege.

"One of them is a woman," Bates said. "She said she had to see you, that it was important."

"All right." Traveler stepped into the elevator.

Bates closed the accordion door. " 'Behold Satan hath come among the children of men,' " he quoted, " 'and tempteth them to worship him; and men have become carnal, sensual, and devilish, and are shut out from the presence of God.' "

"Satan seems everywhere this morning," Traveler said.

Bates nodded. "It's nothing personal." He pushed the start lever. The elevator shuddered before getting under way.

The Mormon Tabernacle Choir, amplified by Bates's cassette player, pursued Traveler down the second floor's marble hallway. He could still hear it when he reached the frosted glass door. Black lettering read OREN G. RIGDON, DENTIST, though the man had retired nearly a year ago.

Traveler knocked. From inside came the sound of high heels clicking across the floor. The door opened. The woman standing there said, "Moroni Traveler?"

"Yes."

"I'm Stacie Breen. Remember me?"

"Jesus," he breathed. She was Claire's friend, the one he'd

talked to on the telephone right after Claire had been killed. The one who told him Claire had given away her son, the son she'd named after him. Not for adoption, he remembered, but for money.

Stacie backed away. Traveler followed her in, closing the door. Only then did he realize that a man was standing against the wall behind him.

"That's Jon," she said. "My boyfriend. I brought him along because I didn't want any trouble."

Jon was wearing a T-shirt to show off his weightlifter's muscles. He smiled, folding his corded arms. But his eyes shimmied as if to say he hadn't reckoned on Traveler's size.

The woman was the age Claire would have been, in her early thirties, but all resemblance ended there. Where Claire had been dark and thin, Stacie was blond and pudgy. Seeing her and the contrast the two must have made together, one attracting men, the other invisible to most, Traveler realized why Claire had taken her for a friend, the only female companion she'd ever mentioned.

He moved into the center of the room, positioning himself so he could watch them both at the same time. The office was bare of everything but the lingering smell of dental antiseptic.

"Why should there be any trouble?" he asked, though he felt certain Claire's influence was about to make itself felt.

"I told you once I didn't know where Claire's son was. Do you remember that?"

"Your exact words were, 'She gave him away so that you'd be sure to come looking for her.'"

"For her and the boy," Stacie amended.

"You told me he was in southern Utah, but you didn't know the exact location."

"I know where he is now."

Traveler clenched his teeth. Claire would have said the same thing, whether it was true or not.

"When things got tough for Claire, she left the boy with me for a while," Stacie said. "I should be reimbursed for that."

"How much?"

"Ten thousand dollars."

"Sorry."

She looked at her boyfriend.

Traveler shook his head. "I think Jon would agree with me, that you should be a good Samaritan and tell me free of charge."

Jon nervously licked his lips.

Stacie glared at her boyfriend. "Some help you are. You might as well get out of here."

"I'll wait in the hall in case you need me." Jon sneered at Traveler before swaggering from the room.

Stacie smiled suggestively. "Too bad you like thin women." When he didn't respond, she sighed. "How much would you be willing to pay?"

"The boy isn't my son."

"She named him after you. After her Angel Moroni, Claire said."

Traveler moved to the door. "I have work to do."

"Don't you care about him?"

"Anyone named Moroni needs all the help he can get."

He opened the door.

"God damn you," she said.

"Before we talk again," he said, "I'll want proof that you really do know where he is."

6

By the time Traveler left the Chester Building, the storm had progressed to cloudburst stage. Across the street city crews, supplemented by a small army of volunteers, were building a massive sandbag dike around the temple.

Still hoping for a cab, Traveler trudged to the corner where Brigham Young's rain-slick statue stood looking down Main Street. There was no sign of movement, no cars, no pedestrians.

Traveler groaned. Water was running down his neck. His shoes squished at every step. He was about to retrace his steps toward West Temple and the car-rental agency when a police car turned the corner and headed his way. Behind it crept a silver stretch limousine.

When the limousine parked in front of him, the police car came to a stop a few yards further on. Traveler bent down. Smoked glass kept him from seeing inside the limo.

The driver-side door opened and a woman stepped out. A Russian-style fur hat, mink by the looks of it, covered her ears. The collar of her camel's hair overcoat was turned up, obscuring her face. Without a word, she hurried around the car and opened the rear door for him.

Traveler hesitated.

From inside a man's deep voice said, "What are you trying to do, young man, heat the sidewalk?"

Traveler smiled at the girl, who stared through him like a soldier on parade. She wasn't much more than twenty, with that fresh kind of beauty that requires no makeup. Her intense stare propelled him inside and face to face with a bull-like, silver-haired man who shook hands like a wrestler. Traveler recognized him immediately from newspaper photos and appearances on television.

"I'm Elihu Moseby," he confirmed. "As for you, young man, don't bother introducing yourself. The prophet has told me all about you. I must say, though, you look too big to be named for our angel."

Moseby's voice was so forceful it produced sympathetic vibrations inside Traveler's chest. On TV and Tabernacle Radio, he was the church's voice of authority. He was also its First Apostle, at sixty the youngest of the twelve apostles, and rumored to be the eventual successor to Elton Woolley.

"They tell me you were once a professional football player," Moseby said.

"I was a linebacker for Los Angeles, but that was a long time ago."

Moseby removed his rimless glasses and polished the lenses carefully on a pressed white handkerchief. "I know how you feel about the past. A lifetime ago I was a general in the army. Would you believe that to look at me now?"

Traveler said nothing; he wasn't expected to. But that didn't stop him from thinking that Moseby looked more like a warrior than an apostle.

"In case you were wondering about security . . ." Moseby nodded toward the front seat, where the young woman was once again behind the wheel. A glass shield separated her from the backseat. "Chris can't hear us as long as she keeps the engine running and the heater on. And she knows me, the warmer the better." His voice sounded loud enough to pierce any barrier.

Traveler said, "An hour ago I was briefed by a man so security-conscious he was afraid to use his own office."

Moseby snorted. "I'm beginning to believe what they told me about you. That you're not easily intimidated."

Traveler answered with a shrug.

Moseby went through his glasses-cleaning ritual again, squinting at Traveler the whole time. Finally he said, "I want everything clear between us. Elton Woolley is more than my prophet. He's my friend. I wouldn't want anything to happen to him. He's depending on you, Mr. Traveler, and so am I."

"I'm not a Saint," Traveler said, "though I'm sure you already know that. You must also know that I didn't volunteer for this."

"That's one of the reasons I'm here. I like to assess a man's commitment for myself. After all, you're Willis Tanner's man, not mine."

"I'm my own man."

"They told me that about you, too."

"Then you know I'll do my best."

"I want miracles if need be. And I'll pay for them. You can count on that."

"Miracles are your business, not mine."

For an instant, Moseby looked offended. Then suddenly he smiled. "I think you'll do, Mr. Traveler. In any case, I'll pray for your success."

He gripped Traveler's forearm. "You may call on me day or night. Succeed in this and my friendship is yours. You'll be in a position to name your own price. But if your actions harm the prophet in any way . . ."

He didn't have to say more. In a theocracy like Utah, Traveler knew he couldn't survive with an enemy as powerful as the First Apostle.

Moseby pushed a button near his left hand. The driver got out and came around to open Traveler's door.

"Do you have any questions?" Moseby said.

"I was on my way to rent a car."

"When I was your age, I enjoyed walking. Close the door behind you. You're letting the heat out."

"I was hoping you could drop me off."

"Hopes are wonderful things. They keep a man on his toes. Besides, I'm needed elsewhere."

Traveler stepped out into the deluge.

"Remember this," Moseby called after him. "There are two forces at work on earth today, God's and Satan's. Since the Mormon Church is doing God's work, those who oppose us are in league with the devil."

7

Traveler arrived home driving a rental Ford pickup with over-size tires. Getting down out of it was awkward even for a man his height.

Martin met him on the front porch. "Take your clothes off out here. Otherwise you'll curl the carpet."

When Traveler glanced toward the neighbors, Martin gestured impatiently. "In this downpour the neighbors can't see a thing. Now get moving before you catch cold."

Rather than argue, Traveler stripped down to his underwear and socks, while carefully protecting the plastic bag that held the missing girl's photograph. "If you're satisfied, I'd like to take a hot shower."

"I heard that damned truck coming for a block," Martin said. "What happened to your car?"

"I left it in the snow on South Temple. By now it's washed away."

"I told you to get something more reliable."

"You told me to get new tires," Traveler said. "Besides, I'm thinking about buying a better car."

"I suppose that means Willis Tanner is footing the bills?"

"Let's get out of the wind," Traveler said. "I'm turning to ice."

He edged around his father and shuffled inside where he collapsed into one of the twin recliners that faced the fireplace.

"I'll fix you a hot toddy, then you can shower and we can both go back to bed," Martin said.

"I'm working."

"I knew it." Martin knelt in front of the fireplace and set a match to the waiting newspaper and kindling. Once the flames took hold, he groaned to his feet, massaging the small of his back thoroughly before settling into the vacant recliner. "Are you going to tell me about it or am I going to have to call Willis Tanner?"

Speaking slowly through his fatigue, Traveler recounted his interview with Tanner and Elihu Moseby. By the time he finished, his father knew as much about the kidnapping as anyone did. As an afterthought, Traveler mentioned his new employees, Mad Bill, Charlie, and Newel Ellsworth.

Martin sighed. "What's rule one?"

They answered in unison. "Never get involved in church business."

"Before you say anything else," Traveler said, "you'd better take a look at the girl's picture."

Ignoring the offering, Martin rose from the recliner and stepped to the window that overlooked the driveway. "If you're going to drive that kind of truck, you'll need a gun rack in the window and empty beer cans rattling around in the back. That way you'll fit in with lunatic fringe groups like the Army of Nauvoo and the Sisters Cumorah."

"What do you know about them?"

"What do I have to know?" Martin leaned his forehead against the windowpane. "This is Utah. If it's not polygamists or new messiahs, it's some other damned thing. They all fill the desert with their unmarked graves."

"These are women we're talking about," Traveler said.

"The crime is kidnapping."

"Just take a look at the girl," Traveler said.

Martin sighed, steaming the glass.

"I'm committed, Dad."

Martin returned to his son's side and reluctantly accepted the photograph. When he handed it back he made a face. "She reminds me of your mother."

Traveler glanced at the parade of family photos on the mantel. His father was right. Lael Woolley resembled Kary as much as she did Claire.

Stepping to the mantel, Martin began fondling frames. "The Traveler family is something, isn't it? We started with pioneers tough enough to cross a continent on foot and end up with women like Kary and Claire." He shook his head. "I should have had grandchildren by now."

"You were the one who told me not to marry her," Traveler said.

"Somebody should have given me advice like that about your mother."

Traveler studied Lael's photograph. "So far, no one else is involved, not even the police or church security. According to Willis anyway."

"That scares the hell out of me."

"I told Willis the same thing."

"How long have you known that boy?"

Though the question sounded rhetorical, Traveler answered it. "Since grade school."

Martin flinched. "My father was alive then. I've been thinking about him a lot lately. Look here." He edged over to the lawyer's bookcase that flanked the fireplace. "Just yesterday I got out the old scrapbook and dusted it."

The Victorian book, covered in faded red velvet with an inset porcelain oval decorated with roses, was a family heirloom. Traveler's mother had kept it under glass for years.

Martin wiped his fingers before he began turning the pages. "Look at this one, my father and grandfather standing side by side. They were short, too." He patted himself on the head. "Like I am."

Traveler slumped in the recliner, always conscious that he was a foot taller than his father.

"Lately, I have this overwhelming urge to get in touch with them," Martin continued. "Take a look and tell me what you think?"

Traveler scraped his stocking feet across the carpet to scratch his chilblains. When he reached the bookcase, his mother, Kary, was looking at him from the scrapbook. Seeing her condemning stare, he thrust his hands into his pockets.

Memory played back her words. *Don't touch the scrapbook. Little boys leave fingerprints. Enough of them and we won't have any pictures left at all.*

Martin said, "I can't remember if my grandfather was raised or not."

Startled, Traveler shuffled his feet. In Utah, *raised* referred to baptisms for the dead, the Mormon temple ritual by which Gentile ancestors were transmitted from hell to heaven.

"I should ask my father about it," Martin went on. "He'd know where Grandad was hanging out."

Traveler remembered Martin saying he'd refuse the offer if anyone tried raising him.

"It still haunts me," Martin said, "even after all this time. The fact that I can't talk to my father anymore."

For years Traveler had felt the same about his genetic father, whom he'd never known. But whenever he'd raised the subject, Martin's response was always the same. *It's upbringing that counts, not genes.*

Martin closed the scrapbook with a loud snap. "When I was growing up, I never gave much thought to my father. He was there and always would be."

He turned away, but not before Traveler saw the wetness in his eyes.

"Even when I was grown up and away from home," Martin added, "I always knew I could come back here if things got too bad. That he would take me in. That's one of the reasons I kept your room for you all those years you were playing football, Mo. Even when you were living with Claire."

Martin put down the scrapbook and went back to the mantel. After a moment, he began fussing with the photo arrangement, which he kept in chronological order from left to right.

"What are you trying to tell me?" Traveler said.

Martin nodded at one of the photographs. "Even now, years after my father's death, I find myself reaching for the phone to call him."

He paused to draw a deep breath. It seeped away in a sigh. "I tried the old phone number yesterday, 3-7775. Nothing happened though, no rings, nothing."

"You'd better sit down," Traveler said. He eased his father into a recliner and tilted its backrest.

"I tried Grandfather, too," Martin went on. "His place on Thirteenth East. You remember it, don't you? 3-2084." He shook his head. "No luck there either."

Christ, Traveler thought, collapsing into the other recliner so hard it shuddered. His father was going around the bend.

"Your mother would have hated these chairs," Martin said. "Come to think of it, I agree with her. Naugahyde ought to be outlawed."

Kary had been dead more than a year when Martin bought the pair of them.

Martin snorted. "Maybe I ought to try calling her. Tell her that we've redecorated."

Did Alzheimer's come on overnight? Traveler wondered. His mind answered with a telephone number of its own, 3-9712. It was Johnny's, a boyhood pal who'd lived around the corner on U Street.

"These days it takes seven numbers," Martin said. "But that doesn't make it right, not being able to talk to the people you love."

"Dad, I'm going to need your help finding the girl."

"I can't even find my own relatives."

Traveler thought that over. He'd have to call Willis and let him know the situation. The job was impossible enough even with Martin's help.

Feeling depressed, Traveler left his father by the fire and

went to change his clothes. While he was in his room, the one he'd grown up in, he packed a change of clothes into a waterproof flight bag. As a precaution, he added a .45 automatic, one of his father's war souvenirs, plus two full clips of ammunition.

By the time he returned to the living room, Martin was standing by the door, holding a hot toddy. "Here, drink this. You need sleep. We both do."

Traveler shook his head. "In case you've forgotten, we've got a deadline."

Martin took a sip. "You should have packed a bag for me too. If this thing goes wrong, we'll both have to leave town in a hurry."

"Are you feeling okay?" Traveler asked.

"Just tell me what your plan of attack is."

Traveler sighed with relief. His father sounded like his old self. "I'll start with the ex-boyfriend, Dwight Hafen, then move on to the Army of Nauvoo."

"The weather's going to slow us up."

"It can't be helped."

"Do you really think anybody'd be crazy enough to kill the prophet's grandniece?"

"Yesterday I wouldn't have thought anybody would be nuts enough to kidnap her," Traveler said.

His father sighed. "I'll take the Sisters Cumorah. There was no listing in the phone book, but information gave me a number, which didn't answer when I tried it, and an address in Magna. Smoot Street."

Magna was Kennecott Copper's smelter town, located out near the Great Salt Lake. Smoot Street, if Traveler remembered correctly, was halfway between the tailings pond and the spill canal.

"Be careful," Traveler said. "Even if these women aren't kidnappers, some feminists believe men are their enemies."

"Do you think they're right?"

"Considering our luck with women, how would I know?"

8

One of Willis Tanner's nameless assistants pointed out Dwight Hafen, who was among the fifty or so volunteers sandbagging the Eagle Gate, a Mormon monument spanning State Street at the intersection of South Temple. The gate marked the original entrance to Brigham Young's estate at the mouth of City Creek Canyon. It now marked an incipient river pouring down State Street.

Traveler waded through six inches of water to reach Hafen, who had the anchor position at the base of one of the gate's four pillars. He was stacking sandbags that others passed along to him. He did it with ease, standing straight, while everyone else looked slump-shouldered and humpbacked.

"Dwight Hafen?" Traveler shouted over the sound of rushing water.

"That's right." The rain was falling so hard it sluiced from Hafen's hair.

Traveler introduced himself.

Hafen grabbed his hand and squeezed. He was nearly as big as Traveler and a lot younger, but the handshake was a stand-off.

"Willis Tanner told me to expect you," Hafen said the moment he let go.

Traveler nodded at an open-sided canvas tent that had been set up on the curb. "Let's talk out of the rain."

"I'm needed right here. Otherwise, I'd still be waiting for you at the church library."

"If this wasn't important Willis Tanner wouldn't be involved," Traveler said. "It's also a very private matter."

"Who can overhear us with this racket?" Hafen answered, but allowed himself to be herded toward the tent.

The moment they ducked under the overhanging flap, Tanner's assistant, who'd been standing at a deferential distance, shooed the two ladies from the Relief Society out into the rain. They left their tableful of sandwiches and dry towels to run for a nearby doorway, while the assistant began circling the tent like a guard.

"Who the hell are you?" Hafen said.

"What did Willis Tanner say?" Traveler folded back the hood of his slicker to get a better look at Hafen. According to the man's file, he was thirty, old for a Ph.D. candidate. Most likely, he'd gotten a late start because of the church's obligatory two-year missions. When Traveler tried to imagine him as part of a two-man LDS recruiting team, he saw Hafen playing Jeff to his partner's weaker Mutt.

Hafen met Traveler's gaze calmly. "When you're in my position you don't question a man like Mr. Tanner, who works directly for the prophet." He blinked water from his eyes. "Is it true what they say about Mr. Tanner, that he's sometimes called on to interpret the spoken word?"

Traveler shrugged.

"He asked me about Lael Woolley," Hafen said. "Is that why you're here?"

"When was the last time you saw her?"

Hafen snatched up a towel and began drying his face. "Has something happened to her?"

"I'm sure Mr. Tanner would prefer it if you just answered the questions."

Nodding, Hafen draped the towel over his shoulders. "It was about a week ago. We'd broken up and I went looking for her, hoping we could get back together."

"Why did you break up?"

Hafen stared out at the driving rain.

"You don't have any choice," Traveler said. "You must answer, no matter how personal it is."

"I'm a teaching assistant at the Y. Lael was in one of my classes." He shook his head slowly as if condemning himself. "They tell you never to get involved with your students, but I told myself this was different, that I knew better. I knew she was related to the prophet, of course, and that marrying her would help my career. But that wasn't her attraction, honestly. At least not the most important one."

He paused to exchange the wet towel for a dry one. "I think I knew all along that she'd never marry me. I wasn't touched like she was." He smiled wistfully. "All you had to do was look into Lael's eyes and you could see that she was destined for greater things."

He closed his eyes. "She had an aura about her, as if something of the prophet had rubbed off on her. I can't explain it really. You'd have to meet her to understand."

"You still haven't told me the reason for your breakup."

Hafen opened his eyes and grimaced. "She said that I didn't offer her enough of a challenge. When I asked her for an explanation, she told me she'd found someone who needed her kind of help."

"Who?" Traveler said.

"I only met him once. It was enough. She was in bad company and I told her so. But I think that made him all the more provocative."

"I need a name."

"By then she'd already left BYU to join some crazy women's group. I told her it was against the spoken word, but she wouldn't listen. She said change was coming and that she wanted to be part of it, she and her new friends."

"Was this man one of them?"

Hafen nodded toward the street. "I'm sorry. I can't stand here doing nothing. The water's rising. If we don't get the sandbags into place soon, it will be too late." He discarded his towel and left the tent.

Traveler pulled up his hood and followed him out into the rain. Hafen didn't speak again until he was back in the anchor position at the head of the line of sandbaggers. "I don't know where Lael found him. He wasn't one of us, you understand. Not LDS."

Traveler automatically moved into line and began passing the bags on to Hafen. The other volunteers looked exhausted, too exhausted to eavesdrop. Even if they did, they wouldn't be hearing the whole story.

"What else do you know about her friend?" Traveler said.

Hafen positioned a sandbag before answering. "Just his stupid nickname. Roo, like kangaroo."

Traveler shifted his feet. The water running down the middle of State Street was nearing the tops of his boots.

"I remember the first time I saw her," Hafen said, squinting at the twenty-two-foot copper eagle overhead. "She looked like an angel. I'm talking about the real thing, you understand. As if God had reached down to earth and touched our Lael. Yet sometimes, there's something else in her too. She said things she doesn't believe just to provoke me. Like questioning the church. Someone who didn't know her better might think it was sacrilege."

"I need specifics," Traveler said.

Hafen shrugged. "Like joining that women's group. She did it, she said, because she wanted to be in the priesthood. Seeing her determination, I almost thought she might pull it off."

"Do you think the church is going to change?" Traveler asked.

"You mean a new revelation, like the one that let black men into the priesthood?"

Traveler nodded before handing Hafen the next sandbag.

"This is the spoken word," Hafen said. " 'Homemaking is the highest, most noble profession to which a woman might aspire.' There can be no further argument on the subject."

"Those aren't Elton Woolley's words. They come from an earlier prophet."

"Just the same, they remain in effect, along with these: 'Without the Priesthood, the male would be so far below the female in power and influence that there would be little or no purpose for his existence. In fact, he would probably be eaten by the female as is the case with the black widow spider.' "

My God, Traveler thought. He hadn't heard sentiments like that since Grandfather Ned Payson retired from dentistry. Only in Ned's case, such pronouncements usually came in the form of contentious questions delivered when he had a drill in his hand.

"What would you do if Elton Woolley changed the rules?" Traveler said.

Hafen blinked. "Do you speak for him?"

"Not in this," Traveler said, his tone implying that he carried the spoken word on other matters.

A sandbag slipped out of Hafen's hands. He retrieved and stacked it carefully before continuing. "It's not for me to judge. It's God who speaks through our prophets."

"Let's get back to Lael. Tell me about her friends."

"She said she wanted me for a friend."

"Anyone else."

"No one close that I remember."

"Did you ever meet her associates in the women's group?"

"She offered but I refused."

"Why?"

He shook his head.

"You must answer."

Hafen nodded at Tanner's assistant, who was watching them from the tent. "My watchdog. They sent him along when I left the library. What do you think he'd do if I tried to escape?"

"Willis isn't a man to cross."

Hafen sighed. "I'm sorry to say, there was a moment when I thought maybe Lael didn't like men, if you know what I mean. But it didn't turn out that way. Not the way she chased after Roo."

"Think," Traveler said. "Tell me about him, anything at all."

"I told you. He's a Gentile."

"Describe him."

"A pretty-boy if you ask me. One of those California types you see on television." Hafen bent over, resting his hands on his knees.

Behind Traveler, the line of sandbaggers rested, too.

"Tell me the truth," Hafen said. "Has Lael run away with him? Is that why you're here?"

"How tall is he?" Traveler said.

"A couple of inches shorter than I am. Five feet ten maybe. Thin, about a hundred and forty pounds." Hafen snatched a sandbag and rammed it into place. "Blond and blue-eyed, too. I didn't have a chance against him. I guess that's why I followed them." He stopped talking to wipe his face. "I wouldn't tell you this if I didn't have to."

"I know," Traveler said softly.

"I wanted to catch them doing something I could use against them."

"Did you?"

"They didn't do anything except drive around in that camper of his. They didn't even get in back."

"What about a license number?"

Hafen looked sly as he dug into his pocket and extracted a wallet wrapped in plastic. He handed it to Traveler. "I wrote it down on a piece of paper. It's in with the bills. I hope you're going after that guy."

Traveler used his raincoat to shelter the wallet while he opened it and transferred the license number to his own billfold. "What made you write the number down?"

"I had some wild idea about tracking him down when Lael wasn't around and challenging him to a fight." He shook his head. "But I knew all along I was fooling myself. Lael would never have forgiven me if I'd hurt him."

Hafen raised his head, opening his eyes against the downpour. " 'They did eat, they drank, they married wives, they were given in marriage, until the day that Noah entered into the ark, and the flood came, and destroyed them all.' "

9

Despite the downpour, a three-man cleaning crew was scrubbing graffiti from the temple wall at the corner of South Temple and Main Street. One word, still legible, was giving them trouble: SATAN.

Traveler marveled at the ingenuity of the vandals; they'd had to bypass a no-parking barrier of sawhorses and then climb a sandbag barricade to reach the temple walls.

Since Traveler was the only pedestrian in sight, he crossed in the middle of the block to avoid the crew. The water on South Temple was still manageable and confined mostly to the gutters, though the driveway alongside the Chester Building was funneling overflow onto the sidewalk.

Bill's sandwich board, plastered with TITHE THE TRUE PROPHET under plastic, formed a tent out front. Inside it huddled Newel Ellsworth. His mittened hand came out to rattle a collection can against Traveler's knees.

Traveler couldn't resist. "I gave at the office."

Ellsworth's head joined his hand. "Sorry, Moroni. I didn't recognize your feet."

"There's no use staying out here in weather like this."

"I got a quarter a while back."

"It's getting cold again," Traveler said. "Could be we're in for more snow."

"Bill says I have to prove myself. Besides, I can't stay inside when you're paying me five dollars an hour to keep my ears open."

"My client can afford it. Now come inside and warm up."

"I tried the liquor store for you, figuring I could pump the guys in line for information. Only I forgot it was Sunday. That's when Bill sent me down to the bootlegger's on Second South. I was the only one buying there, though, because of his premium prices."

"I'm sure you did your best," Traveler said as he helped the man crawl out of his makeshift tent.

"Did you see the writing on the temple wall?" Ellsworth asked.

Traveler folded the sandwich board and tucked it under his arm. "There wasn't much left by the time I got there."

" 'Satan is walking among us,' it said."

"Did you see who did it?"

"A car went by making a hell of a racket. I think his tailpipe was dragging, but I didn't poke my head out to check. He stopped, though. Kids probably. Who else would spray the temple wall? Anyway, my benefactor came by with his quarter a few minutes later. That's when I took a stretch and spotted the artwork. Two colors, black and red. Satan in red. Too obvious if you ask me. No imagination."

Traveler hesitated in front of the revolving door. "Has Barney come in today?"

"You bet. He's fixing one of his Sunday goulashes. Supper's at four."

Angling the board to fit into the door's revolving slots, Traveler pushed inside. Barney Chester was behind the cigar counter, stirring his stew. The iron pot, big enough to hold a three-day supply, looked precarious on the small hot plate. Traveler knew from past experience that the food, like Chester's coffee, smelled better than it would taste.

Bill and Charlie were on the customer side of the counter watching Chester's every move. The moment Traveler joined the pair, Chester banged his wooden spoon on the edge of the pot and replaced the lid. When he turned around, he pointed the spoon at Traveler. "Bill tells me you're working for the church."

"I keep the names of my clients confidential."

"No, you don't. Bill saw you across the street."

Bill shook his head. "I didn't say you were working for anybody in particular, Moroni."

"I can read between the lines," Chester said. He put down his spoon, took up a fresh cigar and thrust it into the perpetual flame burning at one end of the counter. After inhaling deeply, he blew smoke rings toward the yellowing mural on the ceiling. Chester claimed it was his way of protesting the church's Word of Wisdom, which outlawed tobacco, liquor, and even caffeine.

"Why is it you never light up in front of the faithful?" Traveler said.

Waving away both smoke and the question, Chester spoke around his cigar. "What's this I hear about Satan?"

"They're erasing him across the street," Ellsworth said. When he started to explain, Traveler excused himself and headed for the elevator.

"We're serving promptly at four," Chester called after him.

Nephi Bates was standing in the elevator's open doorway.

"Is Barney paying you overtime on the Sabbath?" Traveler said once he was inside the cage.

Nodding, Bates closed the door.

"Barney says you're a church spy," Traveler said.

Bates smiled.

" 'He buildeth upon a sandy foundation,' " Traveler dredged up from Sunday school, " 'and the gates of hell stand open to receive such when the floods come and the winds beat upon them.' "

Widening his smile, Bates plugged earphones into his cas-

52

sette, attached them to his ears, and ferried Traveler to the third floor in silence.

Traveler walked down the foot-worn marble hall to his office. Once inside, he dropped his coat on the client's chair and sat behind his desk. After a moment, he took out Lael Woolley's photograph and propped it against his coffee cup. Her expression seemed different to him, less brooding, more mocking.

Come on, he thought. You know better than to start imagining things. His perception of her had changed, that was all, forever altered by Dwight Hafen's comments.

He tapped the desk in front of her photo. "Do you really want to join the priesthood or were you pulling Hafen's chain?"

When she didn't answer, he picked up the phone and dialed the special number Willis Tanner had provided.

After the first ring Elihu Moseby's deep, unmistakable voice came on. "Yes."

Traveler identified himself.

"What may I do for you, Moroni?"

"I didn't expect the First Apostle to answer himself."

"The fewer people who know about this the better. That's why Willis Tanner and I are taking turns."

"I have a license plate number I want checked."

"What does it have to do with the girl?"

"The number belongs to her new boyfriend," Traveler said.

"Do you think he kidnapped her?"

"Dwight Hafen thinks she was keeping bad company."

"Let me get a pencil," Moseby said. "All right, go ahead."

Traveler smiled at the image of a man like Moseby doing a detective's dirty work.

"I'm waiting," Moseby said.

Keeping his eyes on Lael, Traveler supplied the numbers for Roo's camper.

"Just a minute. I'll have to find Tanner so he can run it through our computer. I'm not sure how this phone works, so I won't put you on hold."

The receiver clanked down.

"Am I being recorded?" Traveler said.

Silence answered him.

Traveler went back to watching Lael Woolley. He wheeled his chair to one side. Her eyes followed him, a trick of perspective.

"Tanner was asleep," Moseby said.

"I know how he feels."

"He's typing in the number now."

Traveler heard keyboard clicks. He moved his chair again and leaned back. Lael kept watching him.

"Something's coming on the screen," Moseby said. "The vehicle belongs to someone named Opal Taylor."

He sat up. "Are you sure? The name I got was Roo. A man's name."

"Run it again, Willis," Moseby said.

Traveler wrapped the photo in plastic while he waited.

"That's correct," Moseby said after a moment. "The name is Opal Taylor."

"What's her address?" Traveler said.

"Fourteen-fifty Smoot Street, Magna."

"Son of a bitch." Traveler slammed down the phone. That was the address of the Sisters Cumorah. Where his father was supposed to be right now.

10

The town of Magna stands at the north tip of the Oquirrh Mountains where they touch the Great Salt Lake. These mountains, part of the western barrier that originally protected Brigham Young's band from outsiders, were gradually being eaten away by Kennecott Copper. What the company's mining missed, its pollution finished off.

It was dark by the time Traveler turned onto Smoot Street. The road, awash from curb to curb, was halfway between Magna Park and the tailings pond. His headlights caught the house at 1450. It was pure Utah Gothic, grim, gray, and diminutive, covered with asphalt siding and a tarpaper roof. It showed no signs of life.

A derelict car, its rear end up on cinder blocks, stood in the driveway. Traveler nosed the pickup in behind it. There was no sign that his father had been there ahead of him.

Traveler cut the engine and got out carrying his flashlight. The only other light in the neighborhood came from a yellow porch bulb next door.

He left a muddy trail as he climbed the rickety wooden steps to the front porch. His flashlight lit up SISTERS CUMORAH, a hand-lettered sign on warped plywood that had been nailed into the siding alongside the door. The letters were already wearing away around the edges.

He sensed that the place was abandoned even before he knocked. The sound echoed hollowly. He tried the knob. The door was solidly locked. Moving along the porch, he flashed his light through an uncurtained window. There was nothing inside but dust and crumpled newspapers.

Traveler was thinking about forcing the door when a man called to him from next door. "You're wasting your time. Those women are long gone."

The neighbor, in shirtsleeves, looked old and jaundiced standing under his yellow porch light.

"Do you know where they went?" Traveler shouted.

The man hugged himself. "I'm freezing my ass out here. If you want to talk, you'll have to come over." He backed into the house and closed the door.

Traveler waded across the soggy yard. As he climbed the steps, he realized that the yellow light was all that kept this house from being as grim and colorless as the one he'd come from.

The moment Traveler began stamping mud from his feet the door opened again and the man waved him inside. "Don't worry about tracking in dirt. You can't hurt this place."

Traveler unbuckled his galoshes and kicked them off before ducking through the doorway.

The man whistled at his size. "The name's Russ Sterlin."

"Moroni Traveler."

"Hell, yes. The football player. I recognize you now." Sterlin, who looked at least seventy, ran a leathery hand through his yellow-gray hair. "This is a real treat for me. You're the second visitor I've had today. Both of you looking for the Sisters."

The temperature inside was like a hothouse. The heat magnified the sour sweat old men live with when they have no women to look after them.

Traveler unbuttoned his jacket. "Who was here ahead of me?"

Sterlin snorted. "He said his name was Traveler, too."

"He's my father."

Sterlin rubbed the stubble on his chin, several days' worth by the look of it. "I don't see how you could be related, him being so short."

"We work together," Traveler said.

"I suppose you want to know what was going on next door just like he did?"

Traveler nodded.

"Nothin'. That's what's so funny. When that sign went up, I figured there'd be women in and out all day. Something for me to do. You know, watching them and all. 'What the hell,' I says to myself. 'You ain't too old to look.' So I pulled a chair up to my window here and sat down to enjoy myself."

He flapped an arm, adding to the room's heady atmosphere. "A lot of good it did me. I damn near got piles. Hell, days would go by before I saw anybody. The weather's been bad, of course, so they were always bundled up and I couldn't get a good look at them. They had to be young women, though, because they were fast on their feet. But they never did move in any furniture."

"Did you tell my father this?"

"Yep."

"When did he leave?"

Sterlin shrugged. "I stopped paying attention to clocks a long time ago."

"Did my father say where he was going next?"

Sterlin shook his head. "It was a treat talking to him, let me tell you. A man my age doesn't have much else to do. Hell, I go to the store, answer the call of nature, things like that. I can hear okay, though, even over the rain and the TV. Just like I heard your truck pull up a while ago. That's when I went to the window, like I used to do for the Sisters." He clicked his tongue. "I even got out my old World War Two binoculars, though I never did get the eyeful I was hoping for."

57

"How long were they living next door?"

Sterlin ran the back of his hand across the stubble on his chin. "A couple of months, maybe a little longer. Too long as far as I'm concerned. A house needs someone regular in it. A family. Someone to love the place. Those women, they weren't really living. They were just camping out."

He gazed around the room where an ancient overstuffed sofa and a pair of mismatched chairs sat on worn linoleum patterned to look like an Oriental rug. "A place needs love and care. Otherwise, it goes to rack and ruin and lowers the tone of the entire neighborhood. Now that they're gone, good riddance, I say." He winked. "That's not saying I wouldn't like someone to move in who'd keep me entertained. Now take a pew." He pointed to one of the chairs.

As soon as Traveler settled in, Sterlin did the same.

"They haven't taken the Sisters' sign down yet," Traveler said. "Do you think they might be back?"

Sterlin shook his head. "The real estate agent's been around here once or twice. The way they let the place run down, he'll have a hell of a time selling it." He gestured at his own surroundings. "With me it's different. I'm too old to give a damn. Besides, you get to be my age your faculties go. You can't see, you can't taste things like you used to or smell them either. Around here, that's a blessing. When the wind's right, your eyes water from that damned tailings pond. Anyway, that's why they rented the house to the Sisters in the first place. No one wants to live around here unless they have to. Even so, when I saw that woman nail up her sign, I called a cab and went to city hall. 'Smoot's a family street,' I told them. 'We don't want businesses and the like in our backyards.' "

He made a gun out of the fingers of one hand and shot himself in the head. "You know what the city fathers told me? That the Sisters weren't really a business because they weren't selling anything but ideas."

"What kind of ideas?" Traveler said.

"I tried to find out a couple of times. Every time I heard one of them drive up, I'd hightail over there and start asking questions. Only one of them talked to me, though she didn't have much to say except that she'd be calling on all the neighbors sooner or later, hoping to get us all to join up and become what she called Honorary Sisters. The last time I talked to her she said she'd be getting to me any day. A week later she was gone for good."

"What did she look like?"

The old man rubbed his eyes. "She was always wearing dark glasses and a big coat with the collar turned up, and one of those knitted caps pulled down over her ears. Of course, the weather's been bad and you can't blame her for that, but I never did get a look at her face."

"How many women did you see altogether?"

"Come to think of it, I never saw more than two of them at one time." His bony shoulders rose and fell in one quick motion. "Stingy, that's what I call them. What's the harm in an old man doing a little window shopping? Maybe getting an eyeful now and then. I mean, what did they have to fear from a fogey like me."

Traveler smiled sympathetically.

"I remember my wife, God bless her, telling me once she was always a little afraid of strange men when I wasn't with her." He closed his eyes and nodded, a gesture meant for his memories. "I remember her saying once, 'I don't understand why God made women weaker than men. If He hadn't, we wouldn't have to be afraid all the time.' "

"Do you have any idea where the Sisters might have gone?"

Sterlin's eyes popped open. "Strange you should ask that. That last time I saw anyone, she was loading something in the trunk of her car. I was standing right there at my window. Naturally when I saw her wrestling with those boxes, I went out to ask if she needed a hand. She didn't pay me any attention at first, just kept fussing with rearranging things in her trunk. I know when I'm not wanted, so I started to leave. 'You won't see me again,' she called after me. 'How so?' I says. 'I'm on my way to paradise,' she answers."

"You mean the town of Paradise?" Traveler asked.

59

"God knows." Sterlin shook his head slowly and deliberately. "If you ask me, saying something like that is blasphemy. If my wife, Mary, had been alive, she'd have given her a good tongue-lashing. My Mary was a great churchgoer, you know. A good woman. Never missed a Sunday. Now look at me. I'm a regular backslider since she was called home. Come to think of it, I haven't been to church since I don't know when."

Traveler started to get up, but the old man waved him back into his chair.

"She said it twice, you know," Sterlin said. "Like I was deaf. Like I didn't hear her say it the first time. Raised her voice, too. 'I'm going to paradise,' she shouted."

He scratched his prickly chin. "Boy oh boy, do I need a shave. If my wife were here she'd kill me. She'd say I was letting myself go. She'd be right, too, come to that."

He took a deep breath and closed his eyes. "The kids moved away years ago. Take my son, Russ Jr. He said he never wanted to smell Kennecott again and moved clear out of state to prove it. Him, I never see. My daughter's only sixty miles away in Provo, but she has her own kids and can't get up here as much as she'd like."

Traveler glanced at his watch. It was nearly six, dinnertime. Most Sundays he and Martin would be sitting down to roast beef with potatoes and gravy about now.

"Look at this place," Sterlin went on. "If my wife saw all this dirt, she'd march me down to the bishop for a church trial."

He winked to show he wasn't serious. "That woman kept me on the straight and narrow. That's the truth of it. We paid our tithe and never missed a day of church. She taught Sunday school right here in Magna, too. Made the scriptures come to life, she did."

He blew out a long, noisy breath. "It's a good thing she wasn't here when that woman blasphemed. We lost paradise, my Mary used to say. Lost it to the devil." He nodded. "Her words exactly. 'The devil stole it away from us, and the church has been working ever since to restore it.' "

Sterlin stood up, rubbing his chin. "It's about time I shaved."

"Could I use your phone first?"

The old man shook his head. "Not on the Sabbath, young man."

11

It took Traveler nearly half an hour of creeping along the overflowing streets before he found a phone, one of those open, seashell booths hanging on the outside wall of a closed Conoco station. By then the storm had turned into one flash-flooding squall after another.

He shoved the receiver under his slicker and wiped it on his shirt before dropping his quarter and dialing home. He let it ring a long time before moving on to Willis Tanner.

"We're going to need a new address on the Sisters Cumorah," Traveler told him.

"Your father called in a couple of hours ago and said the same thing. Moseby double-checked the license number with Motor Vehicles. They say Smoot Street's their latest location, but he's still working on it."

"Did my father say where he was?"

"He's as bad as you are sometimes. When I asked him what he needed, he said he wanted inside the genealogy library to do some research. 'Now?' I asked him. 'On Sunday?' 'There's no time like the present,' he answers. So what could I do? I had them open up for him."

Traveler shivered. "I don't imagine he said why."

"You know your father. Always kidding around. He pretended he wanted to look up a few friends and relatives, but I figured he was onto something about our problem."

Traveler clenched his teeth. There was no point in burdening Willis with Martin's sudden compulsion to visit dead relatives.

"What about you, Mo? Any progress?"

Traveler thought about the forwarding address he'd gotten from Russ Sterlin. He shook his head. Going to paradise had too many meanings to involve Tanner just yet.

"Talk to me," Tanner said.

"Assuming I don't get swept away in the Jordan River, it's going to take me two hours to get home, maybe three. On top of which, I'm exhausted. You got me up in the middle of the night, in case you've forgotten."

"I had to call you out. If you'd seen the prophet's face, you'd know that."

"I'm not complaining, Willis. I'm stating fact. I've got to go home and get some rest."

"Where are you?"

"Magna."

"Hold on."

Traveler sagged against the Conoco's stucco siding while Tanner hummed "Onward, Christian Soldiers" in time with the click of computer keys.

"I can book you directly into a motel," Tanner said. "How about the Smelter Inn, right there at lake point. Where the Oquirrh Mountains meet the water, their ad says. I'm sure I can work out a deal. Your room free of charge as credit against future tithing."

Traveler groaned. "I'm going home."

"I'm just trying to save you time."

"I want to be there when Martin arrives," Traveler said.

"Didn't I tell you? He left the library a few minutes ago. He'll be home before you are."

"I'd better get going, then."

"Dammit, Mo. We've lost another day on our deadline."

"Relax, Willis. I'll do battle with the Army of Nauvoo first thing tomorrow. That's a promise."

12

"Blue Monday," Martin said.

Traveler joined him at the living room window. Rain continued to fall from low, bleak clouds. Streams of water sluiced from the eaves of the roof. A couple of beleaguered sparrows were perched on the picket fence out front, their beady eyes watching the window as if they blamed Traveler for the weather.

Martin tapped the glass. The sparrows flew away. "The radio says it won't stop for days."

"I don't want you driving in this kind of weather," Traveler said. "I don't want you messing with the Sisters Cumorah either. It scared the hell out of me when that license number matched the address you were checking in Magna yesterday."

"What about me? Don't I get to worry?"

"That truck I rented ought to be tough enough to get me through just about anything."

"That's not what I meant," Martin said. "Are you still planning to tackle the Army of Nauvoo?"

Traveler nodded. "If you have to go out, call Willis and have him send a car around."

"Thank you very much, but I have work to do at the genealogy library and intend to drive myself."

"Ancestors again?"

"Like I told you before, the dead keep coming back to haunt me. When you get to be my age, they'll haunt you too. Besides, we have to learn from the past. If we don't, how can we keep from making the same mistakes over again?"

Traveler sighed. "I seem to remember you saying something about temple baptisms."

"Our family's unraised dead, you mean?"

"Are you telling me you want to be raised one day?"

Frowning, Martin turned away from the window. "The problem is, raising can take place without our knowledge. For all I know, distant cousins have been at work already on departed Travelers."

"You won't find that kind of information in the library," Traveler said. "It's classified."

Martin shrugged. "I heard from Willis. He called while you were in the shower."

Traveler leaned against the window frame and blew on the glass until it misted. With a forefinger, he drew a heart with an arrow through it. "What did he have to say?"

"He quoted a little scripture to start with, something about the Angel Moroni making all things known to mankind. As for the Sisters Cumorah, he says it's only a matter of time. He says the First Apostle is lighting a fire under half the people in town to get you an address for them."

"Then all *you* have to do is stay home and wait for someone to call."

"No can do," Martin said. "Jolene, my lady friend, is going to show me the ins and outs of writing up family histories."

Traveler added a C to the heart, then abruptly erased it. "It's your turn to make breakfast."

"What do you want to eat?"

The phone rang before Traveler had time to answer. He raised an eyebrow at his father.

66

"It's no use looking at me. I don't do phones when I'm cooking."

As soon as Martin headed for the kitchen, Traveler picked up the phone expecting Willis Tanner.

"Claire told me to call you."

He recognized Stacie Breen's voice instantly.

" 'If you ever need help,' she said to me, 'call my Angel Moroni. He'll come to the rescue.' "

"Her rescues were always false alarms."

"Except the one time she really needed you. When she was killed."

He tightened his grip on the phone.

"We got off on the wrong foot when we met yesterday," she went on. "You see, it's not like I'm asking for a handout. I have the money coming to me. I earned it. The plain truth is, I took care of the boy for a couple of months right after Claire gave birth. She promised to pay me back for my time and all the diapers and food I bought, but now there's only you to pay the debt."

My God, he thought, the woman sounded just like Claire.

"I don't have ten thousand dollars," he said.

"Come on, Moroni. Claire told me all about you. About the important friends you have in the church. You could borrow from them if you had to. I know it."

Jesus. Not only did she sound like Claire, she had Claire's timing. Willis Tanner would do handstands right now if Traveler asked for a loan, for anything that might provide additional leverage.

"I have photos of the boy," the woman said. "Showing him with me and Claire."

"You said you know where he is."

"The snapshots might be enough to show an angel the way."

"Angel or not, I can't get that kind of money."

"Now, now, Moroni. Claire told me—"

"You tell him what *I* said," someone shouted, probably her boyfriend.

67

"Now's not the time, Jon," she said.

"You tell him, goddammit."

"I don't—"

The sound of a slap came down the line.

"Jon says to tell you he'll have a gun the next time we meet."

"When is that?" Traveler said.

"When you have the money."

"I told you already. I can't afford your prices."

"As much as you can get together, then. I'll give you some time and then be in touch."

She hung up before he had time to respond.

13

The radio had been listing road closures for the last ten minutes. Thirteenth South was said to be the worst, white-water all the way to the Jordan River on the west side of town. Derks Field, where Traveler had once played American Legion baseball, was inundated. Schools were closed for the day. The temperature was in the low forties with some chance that it might drop far enough to turn the rain to snow later on. But in the downtown area, Monday morning traffic was pretty much as usual.

As a result, Traveler was creeping along when he turned off West Temple onto Pierpont Avenue. Even at slow speed, a patch of oily asphalt sent him fishtailing toward the curb. He corrected immediately, accelerating just enough to make the four-wheel drive grab hold. He was about to sigh with relief when his rear bumper caught the fender of a parked car.

He eased to a stop. Behind him someone honked. Gritting his teeth, Traveler continued on up Pierpont until he found a parking place in front of the Oregon Shortline Railroad Building, the address listed for the Army of Nauvoo.

The honker fired one last shot and drove on. There were no

pedestrians on the street when Traveler got out of the truck. He checked the pickup's heavy-duty rear bumper. The metal was scratched but unbent.

His breath billowed like one of Barney Chester's cigars as he made his way back to the parked car.

"Dammit," he muttered. The front fender was sliced open from the wheel all the way to the headlight.

"Thank you again, Willis Tanner."

The car was a Mercedes-Benz. Fixing that fender would cost more than Traveler had paid for his Ford Fairmont, which was still among the missing.

He looked around. There were no witnesses.

Groaning, he stuck one of his business cards beneath the windshield wiper. With any luck the church would pay for repairs. No doubt the measure of their benevolence would depend on the outcome of the kidnapping.

Shrugging, he headed for the Shortline building. Over the years it had gone through many transformations. After the Oregon Railroad fled the state, the Union Pacific had taken over for a while. The structure had even housed the Utah National Guard at one time. Now it was the temporary head-quarters of the Army of Nauvoo, or so a sign said. Small print added that historical renovation was coming soon.

Traveler paused in front of the door to admire the architecture, a mixture of gabled roofs, Roman bays, sash windows, and arches of corbeled brick. Utah eclectic at its finest.

The inside was a single room, as large and as open as a warehouse. Everything—bricks, concrete, and woodwork—had been whitewashed. The one exception was a bright red, ten-foot-high glyph on the rear wall. The symbol, an upside-down triangle with a slash through it, looked to Traveler like a road sign forbidding some obscure traffic maneuver.

A few feet inside the door a line of wooden picnic tables served as a counter. They were covered with stacks of photocopied sheets and thin pamphlets. Each table had three metal folding chairs behind it. At least a dozen more chairs were banked against one of the side walls.

"Anybody here?" His voice echoed.

"We'll be right with you," a woman answered. Until that moment he hadn't noticed the whitewashed screen in one corner of the room, probably there to hide the toilet.

"Fine," he called back.

He began scanning the booklets. The titles, in bold black print, included *Feminism and the Church, A Woman's Guide to Mormonism,* and *LDS Stands for Latter-day Sisters.* Like the single sheets, the pamphlets were also photocopied. All had the slashed triangle glyph at the bottom of the cover page along with the printed announcement, PUBLISHED BY THE ARMY OF NAUVOO.

"Those are for sale," a woman said.

When he looked up, she was smiling at him across the table. She looked to be in her mid-sixties and reminded him of one of the family photographs on the mantel at home: Grandma Dora Traveler to be exact, red-cheeked, plump, and smelling of vanilla and flour. Only this woman had a lacquered bouffant hairdo and smelled of hair spray. She was also wearing blue sweatpants and a white sweatshirt stenciled with the slashed red triangle.

"I'll take one of each," he said.

"It would be cheaper to join. You get them free with membership." She handed him a form that asked for a full page of personal information.

"Maybe after I've read them."

"That's my advice to the women who come in here." She gathered up a stack of leaflets. "That will be twenty-two fifty. Membership is twenty dollars, though that's only a suggested donation, you understand. We don't turn sisters away for lack of funds."

He gave her two twenty-dollar bills. "Consider the change a contribution to the cause." Traveler smiled at the thought of charging Willis Tanner for the feminist research material.

The woman straightened her shoulders and gave him the leaflets. "What is it you really want?"

"My name is Traveler. I'm here at the request of the Woolley family."

Her eyes widened momentarily. "I know a number of Woolleys."

He set aside the literature before handing her a business card that had his name and phone number, but omitted his profession.

"The name Woolley doesn't tell me why you're here, Mr. . . ." She read his card again. ". . . Traveler."

"I'm sure you recognize the importance of the name Woolley."

"My name is Sarah Decker." Her tone was aggressive. "My official title here is General of the Army of Nauvoo."

"Miz Decker," Traveler said, using the old-fashioned Utah dialect for Mrs., which could also pass for Ms. these days, "I'm trying to locate Lael Woolley."

"Why come to us?"

"I was told that she's a member of your army."

"Our membership list," the woman said, her voice rising, "is confidential."

"It's nothing serious," he added. "It's just that we haven't been able to reach her by phone."

"Men like you have been trying to intimidate me all my life. That's one of the reasons I'm standing here."

"Any help you can give us will be appreciated. You can count on that."

"Are you offering me a bribe?" she said.

"I'm asking for help, that's all."

"We're a real army, Mr. Traveler, fighting for what we believe in. Equal rights for women, but within the confines of an enlightened Mormon Church. We see no reason why we can't keep our faith and have equality, too."

"I have no problem with that," he said.

"A lot of men say that, but it's lip service only."

He raised his hands in a gesture of peace. "I have a job to do."

"So do I."

Traveler heard movement behind the whitewashed screen. A moment later another woman emerged from behind it. She, too, wore a slashed-triangle sweatshirt.

Decker said, "This is my chief of staff, Jemma Hoyt."

Hoyt, a good twenty years younger than Decker, had one of those straight-line figures, with no curves and no waist to speak of. She shook hands aggressively, staring him straight in the eye.

"This is Moroni Traveler," Decker said. "He's looking for Lael Woolley."

"I heard."

"Then maybe you'll help me," he said.

"As our name implies," Hoyt said, "we're an army here. We have battalions of volunteers, soldiers willing to take up the good fight. Most days the office would be filled and you'd see them for yourself. But this storm has everybody off schedule. If it weren't for a couple of bunks in back, you wouldn't have found me or Decker here this morning."

"Are you turning me down?"

Hoyt glared at him. "When we say no, Mr. Traveler, you'll know it. Right now, I want to know who I'm dealing with."

He gave her a business card.

"Forget it. People can print up anything. I want to know where you stand on the last of the ten commandments as set down in *The Book of Mormon.*"

He shrugged, pleading ignorance.

"Sure," Hoyt said. "Why should you worry? You're a man."

The women looked at one another and nodded. " 'Thou shalt not covet thy neighbor's house,' " they recited in unison, ' "thou shalt not covet thy neighbor's wife, nor his manservant, nor his maidservant, nor his ox, nor his ass, nor anything that is thy neighbor's.' "

The women touched hands briefly.

"To the church," Hoyt said, "we're nothing but chattel."

"No better than oxen or asses," Decker added.

"Now tell us, Mr. Traveler," Hoyt said, smiling, "what do you really think about women?"

"That's a no-win question if I've ever heard one."

Hoyt nodded as if to say he'd confirmed her suspicions about him. "They say big men have less to prove than little ones. Is that true?"

Before he could answer, Decker said, "Are you married, Mr. Traveler?"

"No."

The women exchanged knowing glances.

"In Mormon country," Decker said, "that makes you a Gentile for sure."

"And with a name like Moroni Traveler," Hoyt added.

"Could we get back to Lael Woolley?" he said.

Hoyt leaned across the picnic table to stare at him at close range. "Okay, so Lael's one of our soldiers. Does that satisfy you?"

"Only if you can lead me to her."

"Why do you want to see her?"

"As I said before, it's a family matter."

"I don't think I believe you. So far we only have your word and a business card. You'll have to do better than that."

Traveler thought that over for a moment. "Look up the church offices in the phone book. Call the information number and ask for the prophet's office."

"I think you're bluffing." Hoyt turned to Decker. "What do you say, General?"

"You'll get Willis Tanner," Traveler rushed to say. "He'll vouch for me."

"I know the name," Decker said.

The women huddled. When they broke apart it was Hoyt who spoke. "The fact is, Mr. Traveler, our soldiers are strictly volunteers. We have no way of keeping track of them, unless they're scheduled to do paperwork here in the office, which Lael isn't."

Something about the way she said it, about the way both women were holding themselves, made him distrust the answer. "Tell me about her, then. Your impressions. What sticks in your minds? What makes her different from your other members?"

"I take it you haven't met her," Decker said.

"That's right."

The women reached out until they touched hands again. Decker spoke without taking her eyes from her chief of staff. "I interviewed Lael when she first came to us. I'll tell you what I thought that day, that she didn't belong here. In many ways she's so naive. The fact is, I don't know how she got through twenty years of life without losing that air of innocence. My chief of staff and I talked about it at the time. Do you remember, Jemma? We worried that we might do something to change her."

Hoyt nodded warily.

Decker continued. "I remember thinking that Lael had come from another world. Listening to myself here and now, I know that sounds foolish, but it's what went through my mind nevertheless."

"What the general's trying to say," Hoyt said, "is that Lael is young for her age. She thinks good deeds and prayer will set the world right. We formed the Army of Nauvoo because we know it takes more than that."

"You're being too hard on the girl," Decker said.

Hoyt shook her head. "An army can't afford to be sentimental. Those are your words, Sarah, not mine."

Watching them, Traveler wondered if they weren't Mutt and Jeffing him. Only instead of good cop, bad cop, they were playing good feminist, bad feminist.

Decker tugged at the waistband of her sweatshirt. "Lael really is different than the rest of us. But there's no use trying to explain it to an outsider. You'd have to meet her for yourself, Mr. Traveler."

"Yet you accepted her as a member?" he said.

Decker smiled. "Lael Woolley can be very determined."

"Stubborn is more like it," Hoyt said, but she, too, smiled. "And very hard to say no to."

"It was those eyes of hers, I think. She'd stare at you with them and you couldn't bear to hurt her," Decker said.

Hoyt pointed a finger at Traveler. "Don't go thinking there was anything sexual about our relationship, just because we're feminists. It's just the way Lael is."

Traveler remembered Lael's eyes in the photograph, large, devouring eyes.

"We did talk about turning her down for membership, though," Hoyt said. "She's thin, you know. Very thin. I told Decker at the time that we didn't want to get involved if she turned out to be one of those young women who persist in seeing themselves as fat and end up starving themselves to death on some fad diet or other."

"Especially since she was related to the prophet," Decker put in. "It was her being related that made some of our members suspicious at first. They figured she'd come to spy on us. But it turned out we didn't need to worry. About that or Lael's dieting. It turns out she's a great one for fasting. She says it gets her closer to God."

"I'd starve myself, too," Hoyt said, "if I thought it would get us equality."

Decker nodded. "My grandmother was a faster. She'd take purges, too, once a month, to clean the evil out of her system. But suffering is out of fashion these days, especially with young people. So you can see why Lael made an impression on us."

"She didn't mind the grunt work either," Hoyt went on. "She always did what was asked. That's more than we can say for a lot of our members."

"Did she have any close friends among your membership?" Traveler asked.

The women exchanged questioning looks. Finally Hoyt shrugged. "You have to understand something about us, Mr. Traveler. We're fighting a war. That's why we call ourselves an army. It's also why we organized along military lines. We have battalions, companies, and platoons, and the ranks to go with them. Lael, being relatively new, is still a private. But as soon as we assigned her to Amanda Ware's platoon, the two became friends." Hoyt paused, looking at her general.

"If anyone knows Lael," Decker responded, "it's Amanda."

"There must be other friends," Traveler said.

Decker shook her head. "It's best to follow the chain of command. You'll have to talk to Amanda yourself."

"Where can I find her?"

"She's in the field right now, on a mission for the army."

"Could I see her membership form? Lael's too."

"That's confidential information," Decker said.

Traveler took a deep breath. "You said before that you'd heard of Willis Tanner."

After a moment's hesitation Hoyt said, "We know who he is."

"Are you sure?"

"That sounds like a threat."

Traveler sighed for their benefit. "There are those who claim that he heads the Danites." What Traveler failed to mention was that it was mostly Mad Bill who said such things.

The women's faces betrayed their fear. The original Danites, sometimes called the Sons of Dan, went back to the days of Joseph Smith. He'd used them for blood vengeance against his and the church's enemies.

Decker backed away from the picnic table. "Something's happened to Lael, hasn't it?"

"Help me find her," he said. "That's all I'm asking."

"We'd better tell him," Hoyt said.

Decker nodded. "We've taken our cue from the mother church. We send out missionaries in pairs, using young women instead of men. Lael and Amanda are one such couple, Amanda leading, of course, as the senior officer."

"Where are they?" he said.

Sarah Decker collapsed into one of the folding chairs while the younger woman spoke. "I made out the missionary schedule myself. They're in the northern part of the state."

"You can do better than that," Traveler said.

77

"Our missionaries pay their own way just like the men do in the mother church," Hoyt said.

"The church has its ten percent tithe," Decker added, "not to mention parents who pay for their son's missions. We're not so lucky. Our missionaries depend on charity. They stay with sympathizers whenever possible. As a result, we don't really know where they are much of the time. All I can tell you is that Amanda has an aunt living in the area. We're hoping she'll be able to use that as home base."

"Ware is a prominent name," Traveler said. "Nearly as prominent as Woolley."

Decker nodded. "That's why we teamed them up together. Someone else might have been overwhelmed by Lael's connections."

"Let's get this straight," Traveler said. "Just what is Amanda's relation to Caleb Ware?"

"His daughter," Hoyt said.

"Does he know she's a member of your group?"

Hoyt smiled. "We made certain of that."

"Who recruited her?"

The women looked at one another and shrugged.

"She must have been a walk-in," Decker said.

"Ware is one of the church's most important theologians," Traveler said.

"Caleb Ware is an archconservative, out of date and out of touch with reality," Decker said.

"That's not what I hear," Traveler said.

Hoyt jumped in. "The man's a right-wing fanatic."

Decker raised a calming hand. "Whatever he is, we don't hold that against Amanda."

According to Mad Bill, Caleb Ware was in trouble with much of the church hierarchy, who considered him too liberal on any number of subjects, including women's rights. Only his popular books, published by the church itself, and his close friendship with Elton Woolley kept him immune from excommunication.

"You mentioned the girl's aunt," he said. "I'll need her name and address."

"Excuse us for a moment," Hoyt said.

Both women withdrew to the middle of the room, well out of earshot. Within a few seconds, Decker returned to the picnic table while Hoyt disappeared behind the whitewashed screen.

"Jemma has some calls to make," the older woman explained. "Now what was it you were asking?"

"An address for Amanda Ware's aunt."

"Oh, yes. Let me check the files." She, too, disappeared behind the screen.

He paced for a while, then unfolded a chair, sat down at one of the tables, and began reading one of the army's leaflets. It was entitled *The Betrayal of Joseph Smith* and claimed that the modern-day Mormon Church had turned its back on Smith, its founding prophet, who had originally intended to give women the priesthood. Smith had even named his first wife as a priestess, the pamphlet said. But the succeeding prophet, Brigham Young, had reformed the church into an all-male club.

Traveler read one passage out loud, though not loud enough to reach the screen at the rear of the room. " 'If females are pure and innocent,' Joseph Smith said, 'they may come into the presence of God. They need no male to intercede for them.' Yet the church today says man is answerable to God and that women are answerable to men. It's known as the triangle concept, with God on top, man in the middle, and woman on the bottom."

Smiling, Traveler finally understood the bright red glyph on the back wall, the triangle with a negative slash through it.

Behind him the front door opened. A woman said, "What's so—"

He stood up and turned around in time to catch her startled look. At the same time, a second woman crossed the threshold.

Traveler glanced toward the screen, where Decker and

Hoyt were now watching him. Obviously, they'd sent for reinforcements. The new arrivals moved around the picnic tables so that all four of them could face him as a group.

"He's here about one of our members," Hoyt told the newcomers, both of whom had stiffly sprayed hairdos above their slashed triangle sweatshirts.

"He says he's looking for Lael Woolley," Decker added, "but we think the church is investigating us."

Traveler started to say something but one of the newcomers beat him to it. "Christ was a feminist," she said. "The men of his time didn't allow women to preach or study scriptures. Yet he discussed the Torah with Mary. What do you say to that?"

The other newcomer continued the attack. "Jewish law did not allow women as witnesses, yet Christ made women witness to his resurrection."

All four women nodded. Decker said, *"The Book of Mormon* teaches us that only the priesthood is valid. All other ministries, Catholic, Protestant, what have you, are unacceptable to God and don't even qualify as Christian. Thus, without the priesthood Mormon women are nothing. Nothing but doormats, as the old saying goes. Doormats that keep their men from going in to God with muddy feet."

Traveler felt a cold draft on the back of his neck. Three more women had arrived.

"You've been very helpful," he said and started for the door.

"Wait," Decker said. "You've paid for a full course of our literature. We wouldn't want to cheat you."

They surrounded him, filling his arms with pamphlets as they backed him over the threshold. Just before the door closed in his face, Decker shouted, "We want to be more than wives and mothers. More than doormats."

14

Ida Woolley, the missing girl's mother, lived high on Capitol Hill. Driving all the way there, even in a four-wheel-drive truck, was too risky, a decision Traveler reached the moment he encountered his first mud slide.

Maneuvering carefully, he swung the truck around until it was pointing downhill, back the way he'd come. After double-checking the emergency brake, he got out, tucked his trousers into the top of his galoshes, and started walking.

The river-roar of rushing water increased as he made his way up Wall Street's steep grade. At the intersection of Zane Avenue, he stopped to admire the view of the valley below, rain shrouded though it was. To the west the Great Salt Lake lay like black slag. To the east, he could see the foothills of the Wasatch Mountains. Once behind that mountain fortress, Brigham had laid out God's city according to holy logic, a master plan with the temple at its center. Every aspect of Mormon life radiated out from the temple hub, a rational progression all the way to the city limits. These days, however, Brigham's vision ended at those boundaries, where the secular chaos of the postwar building boom had taken over. Now the city was called Greater Salt Lake, with over a million people and everything that went with them.

Blowing on his hands, Traveler turned east on Zane Avenue. His feet were soaked by the time he reached the Woolley address. The house was smaller than he expected, one of those bleak red brick relics from the 1870s that inevitably squatted on rough-faced sandstone foundations. Its builder had tried to disguise his work by adding a front gable and a bay window. The woman watching him from that window looked as cheerless as her dwelling place.

Stick-figure maple trees lined the front walk leading to the porch. At the side of the house, his father's Jeep station wagon was parked in the driveway.

Martin opened the door before Traveler had time to knock. "Moroni, what kept you?"

"I don't remember making an appointment."

Martin stepped out onto the narrow porch and partially closed the door behind him, while keeping his hand on the knob. "I was rummaging around the genealogy library and decided to look up the Woolley clan. As soon as I saw the layout, I knew you'd head for the girl's parents." His voice dropped. "They're separated, did you know that?"

Before Traveler could answer, his father added, "I would never have believed it of the prophet's family. It's revelations like this that make me think my generation is the last one to have any sense. By the way, if you'd kept me informed of your movements, I could have driven you here myself and saved you getting your feet wet."

Traveler freed the soggy cuffs of his trousers from his galoshes. "Have you questioned Mrs. Woolley yet?"

"You know me better than that. We've been talking about genealogy. There are more Travelers in this world than I ever dreamed." Martin sighed. "It's not just the dead we're going to have to look up when this is over."

"Remember," Traveler whispered, "no mention of kidnapping or ransom. As far as everyone's concerned, this is strictly a missing person case."

"Just like my ancestors."

Traveler groaned. "Come on. Let's get out of the cold."

"If you're coming down with something, it's your wet feet to blame, not me." Martin stomped up and down vigorously. "A son should learn from his father's example. Don't put things off until you have to seek the dead like I'm doing."

Traveler was about to question his father's sanity when the doorknob was pulled out of Martin's hand. The tall, narrow woman who stood on the threshold was dressed all in gray: skirt, blouse, sweater, and stockings. Her hair was gray, too, though probably by design. Her eyes were like those of her daughter in Willis Tanner's photograph, large and dark, almost black.

"Miz Woolley," Martin said, "this is my son, Moroni."

She backed away from the door and ushered them into a small living room where the rose carpet showed recent sweeper tracks. There was only one window, the bay. The walls and woodwork had been painted ivory. An eight-foot sofa covered with a gold, nubby material took up one wall, two matching armchairs another. The remaining wall belonged to an upright piano so highly polished its wood was mirrorlike. The only other piece of furniture was a glass-topped coffee table. It held a photo album and a year's worth of *Ensigns,* the official church magazine, arranged in an overlapping row like reading material at a dentist's office. A single painting, sofa-art of an autumn landscape dominated by golden leaves matching the upholstery, hung on the wall.

Mrs. Woolley perched on the edge of the sofa, sitting rigidly with her knees pressed together, her ankles crossed and her hands in her lap. Martin settled on one chair, Traveler the other.

She spoke looking at Traveler, who found her attractive in a gaunt sort of way. "The First Apostle called me shortly before your father got here. He says I'm to trust you completely." Her tone said Traveler would have to prove himself first.

"I'm afraid we'll need to ask some personal questions," he said, admiring her slim legs.

She caught him looking and tugged her skirt down as far as it would go.

"We might as well start with the easy ones," Martin put in. "Have you heard from your daughter or from anyone else concerning her?"

She shook her head. "She's still unaccounted for, if that's what you mean. Nothing has changed."

"Has she gone missing before?" Martin asked.

"Never."

"Do you have any idea what might have happened to her?"

She stared at Martin for a long time before answering. "You should know that Seth, her father, and I are separated." She glanced down at her hands, which came to life and clutched her knees. "That's a lie. I keep telling people we're only separated, that something will happen to make him come back. But it's not a separation. We're divorced. I . . . we've gone against God's commandment. That's probably why we lost her, as punishment."

"You mustn't blame yourself," Martin said.

"Be fruitful and multiply, God tells us. And what did we do? We had one child." Her hands abandoned her knees to come together. "It's me, of course. I'm to blame. It was my barrenness, my inability to have a son, that drove Seth to another woman."

"We'll need her name," Traveler said.

"The second wife is Crystal Woolley," Martin said for his son's benefit. "I already have the address."

The first Mrs. Woolley shuddered. "She isn't much older than my daughter."

Martin nodded sympathetically.

Tears leaked from her eyes. "A divorced woman can't remarry in the temple. You know that, don't you? But Seth can and did. Now he's sealed to her for time and eternity. Where does that leave me when I'm called home? Answer me that." She sighed deeply. "I've fasted until I was faint, but God hasn't shown me the way yet."

"Do you think the church is wrong?" Traveler said.

The breath caught in her throat. "I know what you're thinking. That my daughter has strayed because of me."

"There are those who believe that women deserve equal rights."

Her hands swept in front of her face as if she were trying to deflect his words. "I know what they're saying about Lael. That she lost her faith and joined those trouble-making women. But anyone who knows my daughter knows that isn't true. Faith is behind everything Lael does."

Traveler watched her with fascination. Martin coughed to get his attention.

"Tell us about Lael," Martin said, glaring at his son.

The woman looked bewildered.

"Anything that comes to mind," Martin prompted.

She took a deep breath, looked from Martin to Traveler and back again. "This house is very old and very small, not what Seth had in mind when we got married. But my parents left it to me, free and clear. It's one thing my husband can't take away from me. Anyway, the prophet, Seth's uncle, has been after us, Lael and me, to move to bigger quarters. We could even have a suite in the old Hotel Utah if we wanted, near his penthouse. Lael was excited about the idea at first. She thought there'd be room service and things like that. But it's a church office building now, I told her, and not really a hotel at all."

She paused to wipe her eyes with a tissue that had been tucked into the sleeve of her sweater. "I don't know why I'm telling you this."

"You never know what might help," Martin assured her.

She nodded and opened the photo album on the table. Martin and Traveler took up positions on either side of her to get a closer look. The first page contained baby pictures.

"Lael was special even as a child," her mother said. "Just look at her and you can see what I mean."

Traveler and his father raised eyebrows at one another.

As she slowly turned the pages, Lael grew into a teenager. "She's like me," the woman said. "Not pretty so much as sensible." Smiling thinly, Mrs. Woolley watched them closely as to gauge their reaction to her self-assessment.

"Your husband ought to have his head examined," Martin said as was expected of him.

Traveler was thinking the same thing.

Her smile broadened momentarily. Then she sighed and bent over the album again. "Lael never had any boyfriends, not serious ones, not until Dwight Hafen came along. I used to wonder if being related to the prophet didn't scare them off."

"It might attract them, too," Traveler said.

She didn't seem to hear him. "I thought Lael was going to do the same thing I did, marry her first beau like I did with Seth."

Martin said, "We've been told that Hafen and your daughter broke up."

"I don't understand it. Dwight is studying church history, one of Lael's favorite subjects. Even the prophet thinks he'd make her a good husband."

"When did he say that?" Traveler asked.

"Six months ago, maybe a little less. I haven't seen him since, not to talk to alone, because of his health."

"I spoke to Hafen myself. He hasn't seen your daughter for a week or so."

Ida Woolley grasped the album's covers and snapped them shut. "You don't have to beat around the bush. I know she went off with a man. God knows, I saw it coming. I don't know how many times I warned her father. 'Seth,' I said, 'it's the shy ones who fall from grace.' You and your father being here prove I was right."

"We understand the young man's name is Roo," Martin probed.

"Short for Reuben, Lael told me. She wouldn't tell me his last name, which can mean only one thing. He isn't one of us. He isn't a Saint."

"You can't be sure," Martin said.

"Lael knows how we feel about her. How the prophet feels.

You know what Elton said to me once? 'If Lael were a man,' he said, 'she'd be an apostle when the time came.' "

"What about other friends?" Traveler asked. "She must have some here in the neighborhood. Someone she might confide in."

"There aren't many young people in these old neighborhoods like Capitol Hill. She did have one close friend, Adele Moyle. But she moved away years ago."

"Where to?" Martin asked.

She shrugged. "Her parents left the church when they moved, so we never kept in touch."

"Do you know Amanda Ware?" Traveler said.

"The name doesn't ring a bell."

With a sigh, Ida Woolley reopened the album and turned to the last page, which contained a high school graduation photo. Even there, in a studio portrait, Lael's eyes had that same haunted look Traveler had seen in Willis Tanner's snapshot.

Mrs. Woolley touched the photo's surface as gently as if it were flesh. "My daughter is a great faster, you know. She has been for years."

Traveler looked at his father, whose raised eyebrow was the equal of a full-bodied shrug.

"My wife used to fast," Martin said. "Mormon dieting, she called it. I didn't think the younger generation went in for that kind of thing."

"My daughter believes as I do," Ida Woolley said sharply. "Fasting intensifies our prayers. It's a woman's way of proving to God that her pleas are worthy of being answered."

She glared at Traveler. "Don't waste your time looking at me like that. I could never remarry. If I did, I'd have to give up the prophet's name."

"Tell us more about your daughter," Martin said, repressing a smile. "How did she take the divorce, for instance?"

Ida Woolley bent over the album again, spilling tears onto the photograph. "We both went to our bishop to talk things out. I agreed with him, that the divorce was my fault. A good wife wouldn't have driven her husband into the arms of another woman. Even so, I think Lael blamed her father. I don't think they've seen each other in months. You're free to talk to him, of course."

With a sob, she rose from the sofa and hurried to the bay window. Staring out at the rain, she said, "Do you ever wonder about hell?"

"That's the province of someone like the prophet," Martin said.

"In all the years I've known Elton Woolley, I've never known him to have doubts," she said. "But they say the devil has risen. Do you believe that?"

"Who told you that?" Traveler asked.

Her bony shoulders rose and fell in a quick, continuous motion. "It's common knowledge."

"Try to remember where you heard it?"

Her sigh misted the window in front of her. "At the Relief Society's quilting group, I think."

"Anywhere else?"

She shook her head. "You haven't answered my question. Do you believe in hell?"

"Before or after death?" Martin answered.

"Is it hot and dry, do you think, or cold and wet?" Shivering, she hugged herself so tightly that her hands crawled halfway around her narrow back. "I've always hated the rain."

She turned to face them, still holding on to herself. "I'm certain that the devil, being who he is, prepares rain or hellfire, depending on the sinner."

15

"What do you think?" Martin asked as soon as they were seated in his Jeep.

Traveler shrugged, causing water to run down his neck. His wet feet added to the soggy floor mats, which already smelled like wet dog fur.

Martin took off his rain hat and shook his head. "That woman reminds me of your mother."

"Just about everybody does these days."

"Your mother was raised, you know. Relatives from Cedar City down south did it. They had to ask my permission, since it was my right as her husband. What the hell. It made them happy, so I told them to go ahead."

Sitting back, Traveler closed his eyes. He'd heard it all before.

"It doesn't matter what your sin," his father went on, "they raise you just the same. The baptism for the dead, they say, cleanses away your sins and makes your soul squeaky clean."

Martin nudged him with an elbow. Traveler sighed and complied with the expected ritual by asking, "Are you telling me to have you raised when the time comes?"

As always, Martin shook off the question. "As her husband, what if I'd said no? Think of it. She'd still be doing time in purgatory."

"Hot and dry or wet and cold?" Traveler asked, opening his eyes to watch his father's reaction.

Martin rubbed his chin, fussing with a spot his razor had missed. "I see what you mean." He glanced toward the house. Traveler followed his gaze. Mrs. Woolley was watching them from the bay window. "Your mother loved going to the movies when that was the only place in town with air conditioning. Sweating, she said, wasn't ladylike. Smelling of sweat was a cardinal sin."

"Hot, then," Traveler said.

Martin shook his head. "She wasn't much for winters either. I remember she was always after me to make more money so we could go to the coast for sunshine in January."

"A little of each," Traveler said, "cold and hot."

"What about Claire?"

"She went through enough hell while she was here."

Martin nodded. "Fair is fair. She deserves to be raised with the best of them."

Traveler stared at the rain beating against the windshield until his eyes lost focus. Whenever he thought of Claire, her son was at her side. The son who bore the name Moroni Traveler the Third, though he shared no more genetic linkage to Traveler than Traveler did to Martin.

"I can see them now," Martin said, "Claire and Kary raised from the dead to raise hell in heaven." He snorted.

"Claire's girlfriend says she stashed the kid somewhere before she died. She wants money to tell me where."

"Claire was like Kary. They didn't have girlfriends, only men."

"We'll have to find him in any case," Traveler said.

Martin's shrug belied his concern. They were already using much of their spare time to look for the boy, agreed that another ambiguous generation might as well be added to the firm of Moroni Traveler and Son.

Martin sighed, popped the Jeep into four-wheel drive, and backed out of the driveway. He didn't speak again until he was headed downhill toward Traveler's truck. "What would you say to your mother if you could talk to her right now?"

"That's easy. I'd ask her the things you're never willing to talk about."

"That's what I figured. Maybe we should talk before you turn into an old man like me and start wishing you could phone the dead."

"How about right now?" Traveler said, lining the questions up in his mind. Who was his real father? Was he still alive? If so, where was he?

Martin said, "The trouble is, there are some things you don't ask, even of the dead."

"Like what?" Traveler said, playing Martin's game.

"Everybody inherits genes, but not everybody gets brought up by someone who loves them."

Traveler smiled. Most likely, his father knew just what he was thinking, that maybe the status quo was best after all, that nothing should ever be said that might weaken the bond between them.

Martin drove straight through the mud slide, then pulled in behind Traveler's truck, set the brakes, switched off the engine, and turned to face his son. "Go ahead. Ask me whatever you want."

"It's hell having a father who can read minds."

Winking, Martin jabbed Traveler playfully on the shoulder.

"We'd better go to work," Traveler said.

"That's more like it."

"If I can get that damned truck started, follow me to the office. We can check in with Willis from there. He ought to know something about the Sisters Cumorah by now."

16

State Street was running a foot of water and had been nick-named the "Little Jordan" by the time Traveler reached the Chester Building. By tomorrow, Main Street was expected to become a tributary. By the end of the week, experts were predicting that Salt Lake would be nothing more than a maze of canals.

But for the moment, the sandbags on South Temple were holding. The Mormon Temple was safe and the sidewalk in front of the Chester Building was clear.

Traveler parked in the red zone, camouflaged by sandbags. His father pulled in right behind him.

Together, they pushed through the revolving door and into the lobby. The air was thick with cigar smoke and the spicy aroma of hot mulled wine.

Charlie Redwine stepped out from behind one of the impos-ing Doric columns, brought his heels together, and snapped to attention. Slowly, one arm raised to chest level. His fist was filled with panatelas. His eyes stared straight ahead.

Martin took one look at him and shook his head. "You're out of luck. Real cigar store Indians have feathered head-dresses."

Charlie grunted.

Mad Bill appeared beside him to translate. "He says it takes fire and smoke to drive away the rain gods. He says you must light up to save us from the flood."

Charlie, nodding, thrust the panatelas under Martin's nose. He took one, so did Traveler.

Bill struck a match. " 'And the rain descended, and the floods came, and the winds blew and beat upon the house; and it fell, and great was the fall of it.' "

Martin puffed to get his cigar going. "In case you haven't noticed, the temple across the street is on high ground."

Traveler lit up without inhaling.

Bill said, "The devil has risen to see to things personally."

" 'Behold,' " Martin said, " 'their sins shall be upon the heads of their fathers; Satan shall be their father, and misery shall be their doom; and the whole heavens shall weep over them.' "

Bill bowed his head momentarily. When he looked up, he winked. "To mark the occasion, Barney has wine on the hot plate. Be careful, though. Charlie's spiked it."

At the mention of his accomplishment, the Navajo touched the peyote bag that hung from a leather thong around his neck before leading the way to the cigar stand. Chester was behind the counter wearing a white apron and stirring the wine. As soon as he spotted them, he filled two paper cups and set them on the glass-topped display case where he kept his perpetual stock: Chiclets chewing gum, Sen-Sen, and pouches of Bull Durham tobacco.

Traveler shook his head. "Not while we're working."

"You don't know what you're missing." Chester put aside his ladle and leaned back, almost to the point of losing balance, to peer at the ceiling mural. "After my first cup, I saw Brigham Young get on his horse up there and lead his people to the promised land."

Bill and Charlie braced their backs against the counter before craning their necks to join in Chester's vision.

Bill said, "Charlie says they're on the move because his

people are just over the horizon. It's about to be the Little Big Horn all over again. Brigham Young will be wiped out and this valley will belong to its native Americans once again. God's will be done."

Charlie nodded to confirm his prophet's insight.

Gingerly, Martin picked up one of the cups and sniffed its steaming contents. "It's a wonder Nephi Bates hasn't called the police."

Traveler glanced at the elevator, where Bates was sitting on his stool reading *The Book of Mormon.*

"If he turned us in," Chester said, "who would he have to spy on?"

Traveler shook his head. "I'll take the stairs. I need the exercise."

"Before you go," Bill said, "we've got news. Yesterday, we borrowed some clothes from Barney so we could dress up Newel Ellsworth. Once we got him shaved and wearing a suit, he looked just like one of the Saints. Isn't that right, Charlie?"

The Indian, rigid and unmoving, continued to stare up at the frescoed ceiling.

"Absolutely," Chester answered for him.

Bill took a long swallow of wine before continuing. "We sent him to church as a spy."

"They shoot spies," Martin said.

Bill dismissed the comment with a wave of his empty cup. "Newel says there was a great deal of talk about"—Bill pulled his robe up far enough to dig into the pocket of his jeans, extracting one of Ellsworth's three-by-five cards—" 'darkness descending upon the church.' Newel's exact words."

Bill gulped a breath. "Even the bishop called on his Saints to be vigilant." The sandwich prophet consulted the card again. " 'Evil,' " he told them, " 'is forever waiting its chance to strike.' "

Charlie shook himself.

"That's right," Bill said. "Charlie reminds me there was something else. When Newel came back from the liquor store a while ago, he said there was something he had to tell you in person."

"What is it?"

"He said he didn't want to write it down in case someone searched him and found the card."

"Hold it," Martin said. "When did Ellsworth leave for his trek into the wilderness?"

"An hour ago. Two maybe."

Martin pointed at the kettle full of mulled wine. "Had he been drinking?"

"Not as much as the rest of us," Chester answered. "He couldn't see Brigham's wagon train moving no matter how hard he tried."

17

The telephone was ringing when Traveler and his father reached the office.

"Dear God," Willis Tanner said without preamble, "I've been trying to reach you for an hour. Your father, too, for that matter."

"We've been working," Traveler told him.

"I'm sending over a messenger right now with two phone pagers. I want you and Martin to wear them at all times."

Traveler nodded at the extension on his father's desk. Martin picked it up and said, "I'm on the line."

"I can't have you two out of contact at a time like this," Tanner went on. "The First Apostle's been going crazy."

"He's sending us beepers," Traveler explained for his father's benefit.

Martin rolled his eyes. "I've always wanted a mobile telephone."

"I'll have a man at your office in fifteen minutes to show you how everything works," Tanner said.

Martin slumped forward until his chin was resting on his desk. Somehow, he managed to keep the phone against his ear. "We need more from you than technology."

"The Sisters Cumorah," Traveler added. "Plus background checks on everyone connected with the Army of Nauvoo."

Tanner sighed into his phone hard enough to create static. "The Sisters are giving us fits. Moseby himself has been kicking butts to get our research people moving. But so far, nothing beyond what you already know, Opal Taylor's license plate number and that bad address in Magna."

"Then why the need for beepers?" Traveler said.

"The First Apostle wants constant updates. Every time you make a move, he intends to be with you. In spirit, of course, not personally."

"Anything else?" Martin said.

"I'm doing my share," Tanner said. "I haven't left my post in two days."

Martin snorted. "You were the same way as a boy. You never gave straight answers, even when you got Moroni into trouble."

"I've personally been on the phone to half a dozen bishops in the last hour alone," Tanner said. "So far the women I've checked in the Army of Nauvoo—Sarah Decker, Jemma Hoyt, and Amanda Ware—are in good standing, complete with temple recommends."

"Whatever happened to excommunication?" Martin asked.

"Everything said on this line is being taped," Tanner said.

"What I'm asking about," Martin continued, "is church policy. Have you people suddenly decided to allow women to speak their minds on equal rights? You sure as hell didn't on the ERA."

"Temple recommends can be revoked at any time," Tanner replied.

"That's no answer."

"My messenger is leaving now. Wear your phone beepers and keep in touch." Tanner hung up.

Martin opened the office door so they could hear the messenger coming. "What do you think, Mo?"

"That we've violated damn near every rule for survival that you taught me."

Nodding, Martin sank into the client's chair in front of his son's desk. "I had a dream last night."

Traveler looked for signs of humor but found none. "I hope Lael Woolley was in it."

"Talking on the phone just now reminded me of it. In my dream, I was trying to call my father, but I couldn't make the connection. No matter how many times I dialed the phone, I kept getting the wrong number. After a while, the dial fell off altogether."

"Keep your mind on what we're doing."

"It seemed very real to me," Martin said.

"For Christ's sake, switch to touch-tone."

"You can't edit dreams."

"Dad, I can't do this alone."

"If my father were here, he'd be able to help us."

Traveler groaned.

"I remember my father telling me stories about his early life," Martin went on. "He told me to remember them so I could pass them on to my own children."

"Fine," Traveler said.

"The trouble was, I was a child. I didn't know enough to pay close attention. That's why I'd like to call him now and ask him to repeat some of those things he said."

Martin paused to take a deep breath. "Do you remember the things I told you, Moroni?"

"I'm sure I've forgotten some of them."

"We'll have to work on that. Otherwise, one day you'll be having the same kind of telephone dreams I'm stuck with."

"Talk any time you want," Traveler said. "I'll listen."

"I think I'll visit the cemetery today and talk things over with a few people."

Traveler started to say something, then clenched his teeth. He'd do a little talking of his own when he had the time, with Dr. Murphy, their family physician. Maybe the doctor could explain Martin's sudden obsession with the dead.

Martin moved behind his desk, put his wet feet up, and closed his eyes. "Even now I see my father as a young man, though he was older than I am when he died. I wonder how you'll see me when I'm gone."

Traveler closed his eyes only to see Lael Woolley staring at him. He opened wide and said, "I think I'd better talk to the Woolley girl's father before we do anything else."

Martin nodded.

"While I'm doing that," Traveler added, "see if you can come up with an address for Amanda Ware, Caleb Ware's daughter."

Martin whistled. "We're in the big time now, after the daughter of another high official."

"Amanda is supposed to be Lael's mission leader for the Army of Nauvoo. Apparently the army thinks they're both proselytizing somewhere upstate. They're supposed to be staying with an aunt, though I have no name or address."

"It's a good thing I know my way around the genealogy library," Martin said without opening his eyes.

"It would be a help if you can come up with the names of more of her friends, too."

With a sigh, Martin swung his feet off the desk and went to the filing cabinet. From its bottom drawer he retrieved Traveler's old radio, a green plastic Philco with a gold dial. He dusted it with the palm of his hand before plugging it in. As soon as the radio warmed up, static began hissing from its speaker.

"It's time for the weather report," Martin said.

He banged the radio with his fist. Static immediately gave way to an announcer. "Rain is expected to continue for another forty-eight hours at least. According to the National Weather Service, there will only be one day's grace before the next storm front moves in from the Pacific. To date, record rainfall has caused extensive damage. The Jordan River is already a foot above flood stage, as is City Creek, which has made State Street impassable. Overflow from Butte Creek is threatening the Veterans Hospital. If the second storm front materializes, all records . . ." Static reasserted itself.

Martin switched off the radio. "If I'm going to the cemetery to visit family, I'd better buy myself a new umbrella."

Traveler shook his head. "Wasatch Lawn will be nothing but mud by now."

"A man can't shirk his duty. I'll expect you to visit me when the time comes, no matter what the weather."

18

Seth Woolley was a vice president of Beehive Life, a church-owned insurance company with home offices on State Street, easy walking distance from the Chester Building in good weather. Today, Traveler had to detour a block to First South, where a temporary wooden bridge allowed him to cross the "Little Jordan," now a foot and a half deep.

The Beehive Building itself, four stories of red brick and sandstone, was built in 1887 and remodeled over the years to suit the needs of various tenants. It had acquired a coat of green paint in the sixties, aluminum siding in the seventies, and a neon beehive in the eighties. At the moment the structure was being remodeled again, losing the last of its nineteenth-century vestiges—stone sills, lintels, and pilaster copings—to become a smooth-faced modern cube.

Traveler ducked under the scaffolding and into a lobby, where he shook himself on a beehive-emblazoned welcome mat. His raincoat, he realized, had come back from the dry cleaners without its repellency. He shrugged out of it and dripped across the marble floor to announce himself and his intentions to a receptionist.

"I'll have to call upstairs," she said with a girlish sparkle that reminded him of cheerleaders at East High School.

The moment she repeated his name into the telephone, her cheer fled, replaced by a wide-eyed stare. "Yes, sir," she said, "I understand." She pushed a button on her desk before handing the phone to Traveler.

"Mr. Traveler, this is Seth Woolley," a man said without preamble. "You had no business coming here."

"I don't think your daughter would agree."

"I refuse to discuss family matters on the phone."

A door opened behind the reception desk and a uniformed security guard appeared.

Traveler said, "I was assured that you'd make yourself available."

"Willis Tanner knows better than to send someone like you to my place of work."

"There's a deadline involved," Traveler reminded him.

The guard came over to stand next to the desk.

"I suppose we can talk in your car," Woolley said.

"I'm on foot."

"Willis Tanner has a lot to answer for."

"I can go over your head if I have to." Traveler winked at the awestruck receptionist.

"I have to eat lunch anyway," Woolley conceded. "I suppose we could go somewhere."

"I'll meet you at the Mayflower Cafe in fifteen minutes." Traveler hung up without waiting for an answer.

The Mayflower, on Main between First and Second South, had sandbagged a semicircle around its entrance as a precaution against spillover from the "Little Jordan." The cafe had been a favorite of Traveler's mother, who'd taken him there often as a child, not so much for the food as for the cafe's tea-leaf reader. Kary thought the woman had real talent.

Traveler was sipping tea made from a bag that left no leaves behind to read when Seth Woolley arrived. He was tall, the equal of Traveler, with sandy hair and an upper lip white

102

enough to have recently lost its mustache. His camel's hair overcoat looked as if it had cost more than Traveler's entire wardrobe. So did his carefully tailored navy blue suit.

Woolley smiled and shook hands like a man there to sell Traveler a million-dollar life insurance policy. He looked nothing at all like his uncle, the prophet. Even so, Woolley's arrival had the waitress hovering nervously, waiting for their order.

Traveler asked for the fish and chips Kary had introduced him to as a child. Woolley pursed his lips momentarily before deciding on the chef's salad.

As soon as the waitress hurried off, Woolley said, "I hope you understand my reluctance on the phone, but I thought someplace public like this might be more private in the long run."

What he was saying, Traveler knew, was that he didn't want a Gentile, not to mention a private investigator, inside his church-owned office.

"Does Beehive insure only the faithful?" Traveler asked.

"Not at all. If you're interested I can have one of our agents contact you."

"I don't think you'd consider me a good risk."

Woolley smiled thinly. "I have an important meeting this afternoon, so we'd best get our business over as soon as possible."

Traveler poured himself another cup of hot water, then took his time dunking the tea bag. "They had a tea-leaf reader here when I was a boy. My mother used to say that drinking tea when you were getting your fortune told was no sin."

Woolley shook his head. "The Word of Wisdom makes no such dispensation."

"What about decaffeinated tea?"

Woolley waved impatiently. "Doctrine and Covenants says, 'Hot drinks are not for the body or belly.' "

Nodding, Traveler sipped the tea. "Do you have any idea where your daughter might be?"

Woolley twitched. "How would I know?"

"You could try guessing."

"I can tell you one thing. She's putting us through hell, wherever she is."

Like having to deal with Gentiles, Traveler thought. "Maybe it would help if you told me about your daughter."

Woolley spread his hands. "I don't know what you want from me."

"Anything that comes to mind," Traveler said.

Sighing, Woolley leaned back. He pretended to stretch his neck and shoulders, but he was actually looking for eaves-droppers. Because of the constant rain, the restaurant was nearly empty, with no one within three tables.

"As you probably know, I'm a bishop and have been for some time." The man spoke so pompously Traveler felt certain Woolley considered himself slighted, that family connections alone should have propelled him onto the Council of Seventy by now. "As both parent and spiritual advisor, I've counseled my daughter since she was old enough to talk. I thought I knew her as well as I know the good book. But her recent conduct took me totally by surprise."

He paused to take a sip of water. "We, her mother and I, can't imagine what got into her head, throwing over a promising young man like Dwight Hafen. He's a church scholar, you know. Some of us who know him well think he's already taken that first step on the road to becoming an apostle."

Woolley's tone said he longed to tread alongside.

Traveler asked, "Is that important to you, having a son-in-law highly placed in the church?"

"I don't see what that has to do with finding Lael."

"I'm trying to understand your daughter's motives."

"Are you implying that I'm responsible in some way?"

Traveler shrugged.

"I was warned about you." Woolley shook his head slowly, deliberately. "I don't understand why the prophet would trust someone like you."

"The fact that he does ought to tell you something."

Woolley's eyes narrowed. For a moment Traveler thought he'd lost him. Then he took a deep breath and continued. "We brought up our daughter to behave properly. She did, too, while I was living in the same house with her. She would never have taken up with someone unsuitable in my presence, I'm sure of it."

"What do you know about the young man she became involved with?" Traveler asked.

"Mostly what Ida tells me." He lowered his eyes to avoid Traveler's gaze. "I suppose she told you we're divorced?"

Traveler nodded.

"I suppose you're wondering why the prophet's nephew would do such a thing."

Traveler waited for the answer but nothing came. Finally he asked, "What did your daughter think of the divorce?"

Lunch arrived. As soon as the waitress disappeared, Woolley began probing his salad with the diligence of a health inspector.

"I did my duty by Lael," he said without looking up from his plate. "As I said before, I personally saw to it that she learned her lessons well. Too well, Ida used to say. Maybe she was right. By the time Lael was ten, she preferred reading the good book to going outside and playing with her friends. 'It's not natural,' Ida would say. 'She needs fresh air and sunshine at her age, not books.' "

The man raised his fork to emphasize his coming words. "After Lael's first day in Sunday school, she insisted that she should have been a boy. She wanted to join the priesthood, you see, and go on a mission. If zeal and faith is a fault, then I'm responsible."

He pointed his fork at Traveler. "I know what you're thinking, a man like you. That there's something wrong, sexually, with a girl who wants to be a boy."

His stare demanded a response. "I'm not here to make judgments," Traveler said.

Woolley chewed a mouthful of lettuce before continuing. "She felt left out, that's all. 'Daddy,' she said to me, 'it's not fair that I can't spread the word of God, that only boys can be priests and marry people into our church.' "

He closed his eyes. "I remember my uncle saying once, 'You could learn something from that girl of yours.' " Woolley sighed and opened his eyes. "The prophet was right. Lael is special. You'd know that if you met her."

"Your wife said the same thing."

Woolley winced. "What did she say about me?"

"It's Lael I'm after, not you."

"Are you reporting directly to the prophet?"

Traveler pretended to concentrate on his fish and chips. Obviously, Seth Woolley didn't know how sick his uncle was. Or that Willis Tanner and the First Apostle were running things during the prophet's illness.

"Let's get back to the young man," Traveler said. "Your wife gave me the name Reuben."

Woolley stabbed his fork into his salad and pushed the plate away. "Lael mentioned him only once, I'm sure of it."

"What about a last name?"

"I think it was Kirtland. I remember it because it reminded me of Kirtland, Ohio, where Joseph Smith was once tarred and feathered by Gentiles. Maybe that name should have warned me that something was wrong."

"Did she tell you anything about this man, Kirtland?"

"She said she was intrigued by him. Her word, 'intrigued.' He was a challenge, she told me. There was also some rubbish about him being an angel because of his roots."

"Do you have any idea what she meant by that?"

"You're the one with the angel's name."

"I'm named after my father," Traveler said.

Woolley started to smile, then suddenly snapped his fingers. "That's right. It slipped my mind until just now. She said he came from paradise."

Traveler sat up. The old-timer in Magna had mentioned paradise, too. "Could she have meant the town of Paradise?"

"She never said one way or the other." Woolley checked for eavesdroppers again. "I hope you're taking precautions. If word of any of this gets out, I could be stuck as a bishop for the rest of my life."

Woolley smiled as if he didn't believe his own words, not for a minute.

Traveler smiled back. "What do you think my chances are of getting to paradise?"

"Nonexistent unless you're raised."

Woolley signaled for the check. When it came he pushed it across the table and said, "I don't know what this business is going to do to my uncle. Lael was always his favorite. When she was only five, she'd memorize passages from *The Book of Mormon,* so she could recite them for the prophet. Do you know what he used to say? 'Sometimes I think that girl's faith puts mine to shame.' "

"Yet she joined the Army of Nauvoo."

"I've heard that, but I don't believe it. It's another rumor put out by my uncle's enemies."

"I didn't think the prophet had any," Traveler said.

"I'm talking about the ones who say the devil has risen."

"If he has enemies," Traveler said, "I need their names."

The breath caught in Woolley's throat. "Sometimes I think I might be one of them myself. I divorced against his wishes, after all. I hurt him deeply."

"I understand that you were remarried in the temple."

"Now you're sounding like Lael. She took one look at Crystal, that's my second wife, and stopped eating and speaking for two days. When she finally opened her mouth, she told me that polygamy was preferable to divorce."

19

From the office, Traveler checked road conditions with the Auto Club. The way to Paradise, they told him, was open, though some of the old WPA bridges were being closely watched. Driving was not advised unless absolutely necessary.

When he got off the phone, his father was standing at the window, staring at the lighted temple across the street.

"You know what I hate about the rain?" Martin said. "It makes everything so damned gloomy."

Traveler checked his watch. Despite the growing darkness bought on by thunderheads, his usual six o'clock dinnertime was still two hours away.

Martin backed away from the window and sat behind his desk. "Driving in weather like this is dangerous."

"It's not going to stop anytime soon."

"And they call this the promised land."

Traveler knew his father didn't actually expect the trip to be delayed, considering the stakes.

"I intend to hold Willis Tanner personally responsible," Martin said.

Traveler nodded. "I'll probably sleep over in Paradise."

"Go first class and make Willis pay through the nose." Martin pushed an old Western Airlines flight bag in Traveler's direction. "I've repacked for you, socks, underwear, and Willis's phone beeper. The forty-five's still in there, loaded and ready to go."

"Chances are I won't need it."

"I taught you better than that. Martin Traveler's patented rules for survival, borrowed from the Boy Scouts."

"Do you want a safe arrival call when I get there?"

"Don't think I have nothing better to do than to wait around here and worry about you."

"Will you be at home or at Jolene's?"

His father answered with an exaggerated shrug before standing up to display the phone beeper clipped to his pants pocket. "To make you happy, Mo, I'll even wear it to bed."

Both pagers went off at the same time.

"It has to be Willis," Martin said. "He was calling every half hour while you were gone. So far, all he's contributing is panic instead of information."

Traveler zipped open his flight bag, reset the pager, and attached it to his belt. "You talk to him. If it's important you can beep me in the truck. Otherwise, tell Willis not to contact me unless it's an emergency. One more thing. Have him run the name Reuben Kirtland through the computers."

"Is that the boyfriend?"

"I hope so."

Martin tapped the side of his head. "I'll run it through my own computer."

Traveler drove north on Interstate 15, skirting the eastern shore of the Great Salt Lake for the first forty-five miles. Rising waters forced half a dozen inland detours, tripling the usual hour's driving time to Brigham City, where he planned to stop briefly for dinner. But the Weasku Inn, the destination of many a Sunday drive when he was a boy, was gone. In its place stood a McDonald's.

The sight of it killed Traveler's appetite and sent him north on U.S. 89 to Wellsville. From there, he swung east on State Highway 101 and entered Cache Valley, a fifty-mile-long basin bordered by high ranges of the Wasatch Mountains. He didn't need daylight to see the ranches and dairy farms that lined the thirty miles of highway all the way to Hyrum, the largest city in the area, with a population of just over four thousand.

From Hyrum, he doubled back on State 165, heading south. By now, it was nearly ten o'clock. His was the only vehicle on the narrow, two-lane road. The wind had picked up with enough force to rock the truck occasionally. He didn't see another light until his high beams picked out a reflecting sign: WELCOME TO PARADISE, POP. 542.

A couple of hundred yards later, he parked in front of the red brick Paradise Tithing Office on Main Street, where the faithful had been paying their 10 percent since the 1870s. Only one place in town appeared to be open, the Cache & Carry Cafe next door. Illuminated by a pair of naked light bulbs, its narrow, rock-faced facade looked more like a jail than a place of business.

Traveler made a dash for the door. The half-dozen steps left him soaking wet. He dripped across the threshold and into a room not much bigger than a railroad car. It had a six-stool counter and three small tables standing on battleship gray linoleum. A small wire rack next to the door held loaves of bread and an assortment of junk food, potato chips, Twinkies, and candy.

There was only one customer, a heavyset man wearing faded jeans, a red wool shirt, and a wet baseball cap. Traveler's entrance brought the man around on his counter stool. Behind him, a middle-aged waitress with bright red hair and smeared lipstick looked annoyed. "We were just closing."

Traveler blew on his hands. "I could sure use something hot to eat." He was hoping to buy himself more than food. Asking questions now might save time, because knocking on doors after dark in a town like Paradise would get him nothing but hostility. "I just drove in from Salt Lake and missed my supper."

The customer stopped giving Traveler the eye long enough to say, "Come on, Dottie. Warm him up one of your specials."

She pulled a paper napkin from one of the counter dispensers and wiped her lips sullenly. "If that's the way you want it, Kenny."

As soon as she disappeared into the kitchen, Traveler did his best to look sheepish. "I hope I'm not causing any trouble."

"Hell, Dot gets that way when interrupted. There's plenty of time for what she wants." Kenny rubbed his hands together with the same kind of eagerness for information that Traveler felt. "Take a stool and tell me what kind of weather you hit on the way in."

"It was solid rain all the way to Brigham City. After that, it was worse, what with the wind blowing. The radio says it's a record rainfall for April."

"When it comes to records, ask a farmer." Kenny jabbed himself in the chest. "April showers brings May flowers is so much crap. Likely as not, April showers will ruin your crop."

Traveler eased onto the stool, spreading his legs so his knees wouldn't hit the kickboard.

"It's going to get a lot worse," Kenny went on. "You can take it from me. I've been farming around here for more than thirty years, and can smell disaster coming. I can do the same thing with people. Take you, for instance. One look at you and I said to myself, 'Kenny, there's a man who wouldn't drive a hundred miles through the rain for one of Dottie's specials.'" He winked. "Even the kind of service she gives me ain't worth that much trouble."

He leaned toward Traveler expectantly.

"I'm here on business," Traveler said.

"Even in good weather, the only people we get through here are feed and tractor salesmen." Kenny pushed his cap back on his head. "Right now, nobody's buying much of anything in Paradise except sandbags."

"I'm looking for someone."

Kenny nodded. "I haven't lost my touch, that's for sure. Like I said, one look at you and I knew. What are you, state police?"

"Not exactly, but I could call on them if I had to."

Kenny smiled, showing a lipstick-stained tooth. "That may be, but you're still going to have to prove it to me. Otherwise, I'd be a fool for talking to you."

While Traveler was providing a business card, Dottie returned with the day's special, a hot beef sandwich with dark gravy covering everything: the two slices of white bread topped with meat and an ice cream scoop of mashed potatoes.

At the first bite, Traveler sighed. The food had that comforting feel of a childhood lunch at Woolworth's.

Kenny held the card at arm's length. "It says here that Mr. Moroni Traveler is an investigator. What do you make of that, Dot?"

"Maybe your wife's checking up on you at last, Kenny."

Kenny snorted. "That sounds like wishful thinking on your part."

Outside, the wind drove rain against the front window hard enough to rattle the pane.

"If I didn't know better," Kenny said, "I think you'd brought the wind with you."

Dottie, who'd come around the counter to sit next to Kenny, shivered and hugged herself. "It sounds like the devil himself's out there."

"Don't mock him," Kenny said. "Don't tempt fate. You know what they say, that he's walking the land." He winked at Traveler to show that a man didn't necessarily believe what he said to a woman.

Dottie rubbed her arms. "He could be out there right now, looking for sinners like us."

"Have you been listening to old Naomi again?" Kenny asked.

"She saw him when she was a girl."

Kenny shook his head but angled himself on his stool so he

could watch the door and Traveler at the same time. "You never did say who you were looking for?"

"The name I have is Reuben Kirtland."

"We've got a Kirkland around here, with two Ks."

"Don't talk to him," Dottie said, "not until you shake his hand."

Kenny smiled nervously. "Are you willing?"

Traveler didn't hesitate. He knew what was happening, that they wanted to perform Joe Smith's never-fail test for discovering devils. "Shake their hands," Smith had said. "If you feel nothing, he belongs to Satan."

Traveler held out his hand.

Kenny accepted it gingerly. Traveler squeezed hard enough to make the man grimace.

"Well?" Dottie asked.

Kenny flexed his fingers. "He's one of us, all right."

"Tell me about Reuben Kirkland," Traveler said.

"Fix us some coffee," Kenny said to Dottie.

She shook her head. "I won't be party to breaking the Word of Wisdom. Not with Satan walking the land."

"Hot water then. Mormon tea."

"I've got Postum," she said and went back into the kitchen.

Kenny tilted his head to one side as if listening to the wind howl. "She's right, you know. In times like this it's best not to tempt fate." He took a deep breath and let it out in a prolonged sigh. "Reuben's a wild one, I can tell you. Maybe it was because his parents weren't from around here originally, I don't know."

"Are they still living here?"

"They were killed in a car crash. As a matter of fact, in just this kind of weather. Their car turned over and pinned them inside. They weren't hurt badly, but we didn't know they were missing until they'd frozen to death. There were some around here who blamed Reuben. His sins had to be paid for, they said, because he was already smoking, and him only in junior high school."

He held up a hand to keep Traveler from interrupting. "I

113

know what you're thinkin'. You, me, damn near everybody was wild when we were that age. But Reuben was different. He didn't believe in the Lord after his parents died. He stopped going to church. He even made fun of living here. I remembering him saying, 'If this is paradise, give me hell.' Some say that's where he's living now, in hell."

"Are you saying he's dead?" Traveler asked.

Kenny shook his head slowly. "Worse. He's turned Gentile."

"I need an address."

"Some relatives came out from the East to take care of Reuben after his folks died. They were supposed to run the ranch until he came of age and into his inheritance. They were good people, name of Jesperson, but they were no farmers. The place had to be sold off to pay the bank a while back."

"And the Jespersons?"

"They moved back to where they'd come from."

"What about Reuben?"

"It was like you'd expect. He blamed them for losing his inheritance."

"Where is he?"

The waitress, carrying two cups of Postum, returned to say, "You won't find him around here."

Traveler questioned her with a look.

"He stopped in here for lunch on his way out of town about six months ago, after the bank took over. He and that no good Wayne Farley. They'd both been drinking and started shouting they were giving up Paradise for Eden. They said they were going there to find themselves an Eve."

Traveler suppressed a groan. He hoped he wasn't in for a trip to the Mormons' Garden of Eden, which, according to Joseph Smith, was located in Kansas City, Missouri.

"I was here that day," Kenny said. "I got the feeling Reuben was making fun of us again. More than likely, he meant the town of New Eden, thirty miles north of here."

"Who's Farley?" Traveler asked.

"In some ways he was wilder than Reuben even, though

114

Wayne you could excuse because he's not too bright. Shot himself through the hand once playing Russian roulette on a dare. Lucky for him it was only a twenty-two. Anyway, the two of them started running together in high school, Reuben the brains, Farley the follower. You find one, you'll find the other."

Traveler stood up and reached for his wallet.

"You won't be driving there tonight," Kenny said. "The road's dirt partway and washes out in this kind of weather."

"Is there a motel here in town?"

"Hyrum's the closest."

Traveler didn't relish the idea of more night driving. "Is there anybody in town who rents rooms?"

"If you'd arrived in daylight, maybe we could have found you a place. But now"—Kenny tucked his head against his shoulders—"what with all the talk of Satan going around, people want to get a good daylight look at who they're dealing with."

For a moment, Traveler considered using Elton Woolley's carte blanche. But that would be overkill and might earn him a night rooming with Kenny.

Traveler dropped a twenty-dollar bill on the counter and walked out without waiting for his change.

20

Two miles outside Paradise the swirling, wind-driven rain glowed red as Traveler rounded a curve. His foot came off the accelerator. A moment later, the glow became the steady pulse of emergency flashers on a car at the side of the road.

He slowed the truck to a crawl. He didn't see the young woman until he was within a few car lengths of her frantic waving. Carefully, he pulled in behind her stranded car, leaving his headlights and emergency flashers on while he got out to help.

She wasn't dressed for rain, let alone a downpour, but was shivering in a cocktail dress, high heels, and one of those skimpy wraparound coats with no buttons in the front. As wet as she was, she was still good-looking.

"Thank God," she said, moving toward him, touching his arm lightly. "We haven't seen a car for an hour."

As Traveler leaned down to look into the front seat, the door on the passenger side opened. Another woman got out and came around the car. Although her face was turned away from him, she too appeared young and pretty and dressed for a party rather than the stormy Utah outback.

"What's wrong with your car?" he said.

The driver pulled on his arm. When he turned to face her, the point of her high-heeled shoe caught him between the legs.

Gasping, he went down so hard he bit his tongue. Pain and self-preservation curled him into a ball. The pointed toe struck again, searing his ear before he had time to cover up more completely. He tasted blood.

"It's my turn, sister," the other one said.

His head rocked under the impact of another shoe-point.

"How do you like it?"

He didn't answer, didn't want to expose his face or his tongue to further damage.

"It's only fair," his attacker said, "paying a man back for taking advantage of women all his life."

He panted through clenched teeth, while a distant part of his brain marveled at the quality of women's shoes. Were the toes reinforced, he wondered, like steel-tipped workman's boots?

He tightened his fetal curl when a toe began probing for a vital spot. Even so, the shoe found a place that made him groan.

"Do you hear me, Mr. Traveler? Or do you prefer Moroni?"

Somehow that made him mad, that they knew his name while remaining anonymous.

"If you don't answer the question, we'll play footsies until you do."

What the hell, he thought, and mumbled, "Yes, I hear you."

"Well then, the Sisters Cumorah say hello."

A toe prodded him.

"Hello," he said thickly.

"When we say goodbye, we mean it. The Sisters don't want to see you ever again. Do you understand, Moroni?"

"Yes."

"You're going to forget all about us, aren't you?"

When Traveler shook his head, they continued to kick him until his world was nothing but pain and the taste of blood.

117

21

Traveler's head began to beep. He reached for the alarm clock, found only a handful of mud, and tried to go back to sleep. The sound persisted. It had to be the phone. He was groping for it when the realization hit him. The pain was fading, deadened by the cold steady rain.

He opened his eyes and saw nothing but blackness. If they'd taken his truck, he was a goner.

The phone beeper Willis Tanner had given him kept raising hell.

Groaning, Traveler worked his leaden arms under himself and sat up, producing pins-and-needles pain everywhere at once. A good sign, he reminded himself, as he attempted to stand up. It took him three tries to make it. Even then, he might not have stayed upright if his outstretched hand hadn't found the truck's grille. He caught hold and held on, shuffling his feet to get the blood circulating. When the pins and needles turned into knives, he felt his way along the fender to the passenger door. His fingers responded like swollen sausages when he tried to work the handle. Had they locked the door and taken his keys? Think. Only one thing came to mind, that he'd left the truck running with its lights on and the keys in the ignition.

He sucked his fingers. They didn't so much as tingle. He took a deep breath, stored it long enough to warm up, then blew on them. He did that several times, until finally the thumb responded enough to work the mechanism. Opening the door and climbing inside was exhausting. But he knew better than to give in to temptation and lie down on the upholstery.

Instead, he inched across the bench seat until he was behind the wheel. Panting raggedly, he felt for the ignition. The key-ring rattle was like a shot of oxygen. He straightened his shoulders and turned the key. The engine started immediately. The headlights came on, revealing the telephone poles that had transmitted Willis's miraculous beeps.

He switched the heater to its highest setting and headed for the town of Hyrum.

Traveler checked into the Zion's Tourist Lodge, a U-shaped court of 1940s cabins just off Main Street. Only after a long hot shower did he feel up to calling Willis Tanner.

"Mo," Tanner said, his voice rising sharply, "I've been trying to get you for two hours."

"I've still got my teeth, not to mention my balls."

"All hell has broken loose," Tanner said.

"I damn near died of exposure."

"Listen to me, Mo. This is important. The Sisters Cumorah called the newspapers and every TV station in town to announce they're holding Lael Woolley for ransom."

Traveler fingered his swollen ear. It felt like a catcher's mitt.

"So far, the press is cooperating, but sooner or later some wire service will get hold of the story and then we're in the soup."

"Are you through, Willis?"

"The First Apostle wants you back here on the double."

"Anything else?"

"What's wrong with you?" Tanner said. "Haven't you been listening?"

"Your turn, Willis. I've traced Lael's boyfriend. His name is Reuben Kirkland. I think he lives in the town of New Eden."

"He's not important anymore. It's the Sisters Cumorah who have the girl. Otherwise, how would they know she's missing?"

Traveler wet his lips. "What do you want me to do?"

"We've tracked down the real estate agent who's handling the house in Magna. When Opal Taylor rented it for the Sisters Cumorah, she had to give references. You'll never guess who they were."

"I'm tired, Willis."

"Members of the Army of Nauvoo, that's who. Sarah Decker and our Lael Woolley."

"Did the agent contact either of them?"

"He didn't bother."

"Then how—"

"We're holding the Decker woman right now. I've got Moseby's backing on this. We'll round up the army's entire membership if we have to."

"Come on, Willis. You don't have police powers. Not yet anyway."

"You'd better know this, Mo. We'll place them under threat of excommunication if necessary. The fact is, there are those here in this office right now who advocate force if we meet any kind of resistance."

"Do you mean Moseby?"

"You know what's at stake here, besides a girl's life. Our vision. Everything our forefathers fought for. Protecting that is all that counts."

"I want it spelled out, Willis."

"If the Decker woman won't talk of her own free will, then other measures will have to be considered."

"Not by me."

"We're holding her for you right now. Moseby wants you to question her."

Traveler took a deep breath. His groin throbbed; his head ached. The thought of driving back to Salt Lake tonight intensified the nausea he'd felt ever since being kicked. "It will take me three hours, maybe four."

"She's staying with your father, under guard."

"Goddammit, Willis, that's kidnapping. I don't want Martin in the middle of something like that."

"The sooner you're back here, the sooner we can let her go."

22

It was nearly dawn when Traveler reached home. By then exhaustion had taken the edge off his anger, though his groin continued to throb along with several other points of interest.

The moment he stepped out of the truck he felt chilled to the bone. The rain had turned slushy, on the verge of becoming snow again, but was still melting when it hit the ground.

Traveler was fantasizing about hot coffee and a change of clothes when Willis Tanner came around the side of the house to intercept him on the front porch.

"I thought I'd warn you," Tanner whispered. "The First Apostle is waiting inside."

Traveler stomped his feet on the doormat. "Let's get this over with. I want Mrs. Decker out of here as quickly as possible."

"Don't look at me like that, Moroni. We brought her here for your convenience."

"Tell the judge that when we're arrested for kidnapping."

"Count on it. Mrs. Decker won't file charges. She knows excommunication would forfeit her soul."

The porch light came on an instant before the front door opened.

"Come in and get warm," Elihu Moseby announced in his tabernacle voice.

Traveler steeled himself with a quick breath and crossed the threshold. Moseby immediately grasped his hand and led him around the recliners to the fireplace, where a log was blazing fiercely.

"I built the fire myself," Moseby said. "My Boy Scout training is finally paying off."

Martin, who was seated stiffly on the horsehair sofa, one of Kary's treasures, raised his eyebrows but said nothing. He looked as weary as Traveler felt.

Perched next to Martin was Moseby's driver. Now that her hat and scarf weren't in the way, Traveler saw that she was younger than he'd first thought. Twenty-five, he guessed, despite the careful camouflage of a well-tailored, matronly suit. She was staring back at him with fervent eyes.

"Good heavens." Moseby reached out as if to touch Traveler's face then caught himself and began rubbing his own cheek sympathetically. "You look like you've been in a fight."

Traveler nodded at Tanner, who was standing just inside the door. "I tried to tell Willis that on the phone. I was getting close to—" Traveler broke off to glance at Moseby's driver.

"It's all right," Moseby said. "You can speak in front of Chris."

"I was getting close to Lael's boyfriend when I ran into trouble. That ought to tell us something."

Moseby waved away the suggestion. "Let's stick to the Sisters Cumorah. Even as we speak, our bishops and missionaries are out looking for them. Even the Women's Relief Society is out in force."

He pointed a finger at the fireplace. His voice rose dramatically as it did every Sunday on Tabernacle Radio when he made his weekly pronouncement on theology. "Because of these followers of Satan who call themselves the Sisters Cumorah, the newspapers are raising hell. If word of the ransom demand gets out, our church may never recover."

"I understand the stakes," Traveler said. "But that doesn't justify involving my father in a crime."

Moseby made a show of examining the family photos on the mantel above the fireplace. "I looked you up in the genealogy library. The Travelers go back with us, all the way to Nauvoo and the trek west. Compared to your ancestors, I'm a latecomer."

He stared Traveler in the eye. "God has spoken to our prophet and he has passed the word on to me. No crime has been committed in this house. You have my word."

"Sarah Decker is here as a volunteer," Tanner put in.

"Volunteer or not," Moseby said, "it's obvious to me that Sister Decker and her so-called army are accomplices in the girl's disappearance. The worry they've caused the prophet is unforgivable. Frankly, considering his health, I'm amazed it hasn't killed him already."

Moseby stepped back from the fire, which was causing steam to rise from the front of Traveler's jeans, before continuing. "The longer this goes on, the more I fear for the prophet. I've had Willis make that clear to Sister Decker already. We've given her time to think things over, to contemplate her sins. Now it's up to you, Moroni, to get her help."

The First Apostle sighed deeply. "We must reunite Lael and the prophet quickly. Without such a reunion, I fear he won't last the week. You're a strong man, Moroni. Your being with us, you who are named for an angel, cannot be a coincidence. God has put us in your hands. I'm sure of it. You must do what has to be done."

Traveler didn't like the sound of that. Neither did Martin, judging by the look on his face.

"Have you spoken to Mrs. Decker yourself?" Traveler said.

Moseby nodded at Tanner. "I had no part in bringing her here. Details like that I leave to Willis."

"She's a church member in good standing," Traveler said. "She told me so herself. If the First Apostle questioned her, she'd never be able to lie."

Moseby shook his head. "Brother Tanner questioned our

Sister before bringing her here. We must leave it at that in case there are any repercussions."

"Such as?"

"There should be no violence," Moseby said. "I made that clear to Willis. Coercion, I told him, is a sin, even in a good cause, and must be explained to God one day."

The apostle shifted his weight. Chris, his driver, rose and moved to the front door, ready to open it for him.

He signaled her to wait there before turning back to Traveler. "I understand that Sister Decker claims to be innocent. If she persists in that, give her my blessing but remind her that I've already convened a bishop's court to take up the matter of temple recommends for her entire army. Without entry to God's house, she is lost to her husband and her family for time and eternity."

"She must know the stakes already," Traveler said.

"Listen to Doctrine and Covenants as set down by our first prophet, Joseph Smith. 'Let thine anger be kindled against our enemies; and, in the fury of thine heart, with thy sword avenge us of our wrongs.' "

As if on cue, Chris opened the door. Moseby strode from the house. She nodded at Traveler, almost a bow, and followed in the apostle's wake.

The moment the door closed, Traveler made a grab for Tanner, who ducked out of reach and collapsed into one of the recliners.

"Take a look at this, Mo, before you lose your temper." Tanner handed Traveler a canceled check. "It's made out to Sarah Decker and the Army of Nauvoo." He pointed to the signature line. "Look for yourself. It's signed by Opal Taylor for the Sisters Cumorah. One thousand dollars."

Traveler examined the check briefly before handing it on to his father.

"Did you have a search warrant to get this?" Martin asked. Tanner shrugged.

"Your evidence isn't admissible in court."

"A bishop's court answers only to God," Tanner said.

Martin rose from the sofa, handed the check back to Willis, and said, "I had them put Mrs. Decker in your room, Moroni."

"We've got guards on the perimeter," Tanner added.

"My father and I will talk to her alone," Traveler told him.

23

Sarah Decker was sitting on the cold linoleum floor in Traveler's room. The down comforter Kary had made for his bed was wrapped tightly around her. When Traveler and Martin knelt beside the woman, she began rocking back and forth, humming atonally. Her eyes were open and staring at them, though Traveler had the feeling she saw nothing but her own demons.

"It's all right," he said.

Between Martin and himself, they lifted Mrs. Decker to her feet and helped her to the desk chair, the same one Traveler had carved his name on when he was twelve. The maple desktop still bore the marks of his first experiments with a chemistry set, a disappointing Christmas gift because it had the formula for gunpowder but not the ingredients.

"I'll fix some tea," Martin said.

"No," she said so emphatically that Traveler thought she feared sinning against the Word of Wisdom.

Her hand crept out from beneath the comforter and reached for Martin. When she caught hold of him, she sighed. "Stay with me." She nodded at Traveler. "He's too young to understand."

"I've tried to teach him the old ways, but you know how children are. They don't listen until it's too late, until we're not around to tell them anymore."

Out of her line of sight, Traveler made a face at his father.

"My son has reminded me that we don't have much time," Martin told the woman. "You must tell us everything, otherwise we won't be able to do anything for you."

"My husband and I are sealed through time and eternity," she said, beginning to rock again. "You can't restore that seal once it's broken."

Traveler smiled reassuringly; he'd be in a position to do just about anything if he found Lael before the deadline. On the other hand, if word spread about the kidnapping and the revelation for ransom, Sarah Decker and her followers could be in danger of losing more than their souls.

"If you help," he said, "I promise to go to the prophet himself on your behalf."

She stopped rocking to stare up at him. Several seconds went by before she spoke. "I believe you. Whether or not that will save me, I don't know."

"Tell us about the Sisters Cumorah," Traveler said.

Mrs. Decker wet her lips. "The first I heard about them was from some of our younger members."

"From Lael?"

"It could have been. I'm not sure." She blinked at Traveler. "You wouldn't be making all this fuss, you and the First Apostle, if something hadn't happened to her."

"It's best if you just answer the questions."

The woman shivered. "Dear God. I knew it."

"Please," Martin said. "We have a deadline."

She drew a quick breath. "After learning about the Sisters Cumorah, Jemma Hoyt and I decided there was strength in numbers. We tried to contact them, figuring to join forces. We telephoned several times. The one time we got through, we spoke with a woman named Opal Taylor. We invited her to our meetings but she never showed up."

Traveler squatted on his heels to bring himself down to Mrs.

Decker's level. "There are rumors that the Army of Nauvoo, your army, and the Sisters Cumorah have already joined forces."

"Not true."

"Do you recognize this check?" he said.

She shook her head. "Did you see the First Apostle?"

Traveler nodded.

"Did you look into his eyes?"

Traveler nodded again.

"His word is almost the equal of the prophet's. If the First Apostle speaks against me, the faithful will have no choice. Family and friends will shun me. When my husband and I are dead, he won't call me to heaven."

"You endorsed the check," Traveler said.

Tears sprang from her eyes and began rolling down her cheeks.

"Did you get it from Opal Taylor?"

"We have student missionaries on the BYU campus in Provo. It was given to one of them."

"I need the names of those missionaries."

She tugged at the comforter, tightening it around her. "If I tell you, you'll go after them."

"You don't have any choice."

She sighed. "We never had a donation of more than a hundred dollars before that check arrived. That's why I remember it so clearly, the day Lael Woolley and Amanda Ware brought it in. They were so proud. They'd been soliciting all day, getting nothing more than small change for their efforts until the woman appeared with the check."

She paused to catch her breath. "That's when campus security showed up. The girls would have been arrested if it hadn't been for Amanda's father, Caleb Ware. He's a member of the BYU faculty, though he doesn't always teach classes."

She looked at Traveler. "After you came to see us at army headquarters, I tried to contact Amanda, but she'd disappeared too. I even called her father, but he told me not to worry. That's it. That's all I know."

Traveler looked at his father.

"I believe her, Mo," Martin said.

"I do too, so we'd better get her out of here."

"The sooner the better. I've got work to do in Provo."

Traveler shook his head. "We should be together when we interview Caleb Ware."

"Who said anything about him? I'm going to visit Grandfather's grave."

"Stop playing games with me," Mrs. Decker said, shedding the comforter. "Tell me what's happened to Lael."

Martin went to the patio door and opened it. "We can get her out this way."

"To hell with that," Traveler said. "We're not sneaking out of our own house."

"What about Willis?"

"He won't interfere as long as he needs us."

"Where are we going?" she said.

"If I were you," Traveler answered, "I'd leave the state for a while."

"We'd do the same thing if we were smart," Martin added.

24

After reuniting Sarah Decker and her chief of staff, Jemma Hoyt, Traveler and his father snatched a couple of hours sleep before leaving for Provo. Morning traffic and continued rain turned the forty-mile trip on Interstate 15 into two hours of white-knuckled driving. By the time they neared Cascade Mountain, whose eleven-thousand-foot summit overlooked the BYU campus, the rain had reached cloudburst stage. The windshield wipers were useless, even at their highest speed.

Traveler was about to pull his father's Jeep Cherokee over to the shoulder of the road when an exit sign appeared, their exit.

"Thank God," Martin said with an exaggerated sigh.

"You're welcome to drive back," Traveler said.

"We'll see after you drop me off at the cemetery."

"What would you do if I actually did it?"

Martin snorted. "Sometimes you remind me of Grandfather Payson. You're both great ones for talking. Of course that's why I'd like to talk things out with him."

Traveler concentrated on getting them off the highway.

"Grandad was a powder monkey when he was only eighteen," Martin continued when they were safely on surface streets. "He worked the silver mines in Park City. All that's gone now, of course, turned into a ski resort and tourist trap."

"I remember listening to his stories when I was a kid, but I don't recall anything about him being a powder monkey."

"Exactly my point. Memories fail. That's why you have to get your information from the horse's mouth whenever possible."

"All right," Traveler said. "Which way do I turn for the cemetery?"

"Who can see in this downpour?"

"The campus is to the right, I know that. City Cemetery must be to the left."

"I'm not crazy yet," Martin said. "Now take a right and stop pretending you believe me about going to the cemetery."

Traveler fought off a smile as he turned onto University Avenue. Their appointment wasn't actually on campus but at a nearby LDS ward house, one of those utilitarian brick and concrete structures that the church had duplicated all over the country. Pragmatic Mormon architecture, Martin called it, right down to a meeting hall that converted into a basketball floor.

Caleb Ware, dressed in gym shorts and sneakers, was shooting baskets when they entered. Traveler recognized him from the dust jacket photograph on his latest book, *Mormon Evolution*. Ware's shaved head was his trademark.

"Don't drip water on the floor," he called to them before sinking a jump shot from the three-point line.

After retrieving the ball, he dribbled over to meet them near the rollaway pulpit. He was breathing hard. His photo had made him look tall; in person he wasn't more than five-five.

Traveler introduced himself and his father.

Ware shook hands. "It's true what they say, you know. Exercise chases away the demons that haunt us."

Traveler had heard the same thing when he played church-league basketball, only usually it was put more simply: *A healthy soul needs a healthy body.*

"What demons?" Martin asked.

"Look around you, at the weather, for instance. They're calling it a hundred-year rain for lack of anything better. I call it a sign. The devil may not have risen, but his handiwork is everywhere."

Martin rolled his eyes.

"When we spoke on the phone," Traveler said, "you agreed to meet us without any explanation on our part. Why was that?"

"Elton Woolley is my friend. He trusts me completely."

Traveler mulled that over. Willis Tanner had assured him that no one outside himself and the apostles knew of the kidnapping and ransom.

"Have you spoken to the prophet recently?" Martin asked.

"We have conferred daily for years."

Traveler said, "I was told he's too ill to see or talk to anyone."

"Considering those around him with their old-fashioned views, he needs a fresh voice." Ware moved close to Traveler and stared up at him. "What are you, six-four?"

"Not quite."

"Strip down and take off your shoes and we can play a little one-on-one."

"I thought we already were."

"Elton was right about you," Ware said.

Traveler shrugged. "We need to speak with your daughter, Amanda."

Ware waved away the comment. "Before this trouble, there was talk of a new revelation."

Traveler and his father exchanged glances.

"Not among laymen like yourself, of course, but among scholars. It was our way of launching a trial balloon, just like politicians do. As you can imagine, word of it caused a great deal of consternation. It was shortly after that, that these rumors began. Satan has risen, things like that. Do you believe it?"

"What do *you* believe?" Martin said.

Instead of answering, Ware whirled around to face the basket. He dribbled once, then sighted over the ball as if contemplating a long shot. "Change can be dangerous to a church. Fatal even. Do you remember the uproar when black men were allowed into the priesthood?"

Traveler and Martin nodded at the man's back.

"When women asked for the same consideration," Ware went on, "the prophet said never. That was his word, never. Since he spoke for God on earth that was the end of it. But we have a new prophet now. Will God tell him something different?"

He looked over his shoulder as if questioning Traveler.

"You're the expert," Traveler said.

"We've been taught that man is answerable to God, and that women are answerable to men. Yet isn't man generic? Isn't man the same as mankind?"

Ware spun the ball in his hands. "God has given us Elton Woolley. Thus, if he makes a change, that is the way God wants it."

Without warning, he charged the basket but lost control of his dribble at the last minute and missed a lay-up. When he returned, his bald head shone with sweat.

"On the other hand," he said, "God must know about these rumors. If they are true, if the devil has risen, then God must fight him."

Ware looked down at the ball in his hands and shook his head. "Forgive me. I've been wrestling with this all day. I thought sounding out someone might help, but I'm afraid only the prophet can help me now."

He wiped his brow with a forearm. "Now, about my daughter. She and Lael have been friends since childhood."

"I was told they met at the Army of Nauvoo," Traveler said.

Ware sighed. "I'm afraid Lael Woolley learned of the Army of Nauvoo from my daughter. When Amanda told me of this, I urged her to keep an eye on Lael. You see, that girl isn't like the rest of us."

Traveler shifted his feet in the puddle he'd created on the floor around the pulpit.

Ware looked down at the spreading pool and shook his head. "There are those who would have my daughter excommunicated for her membership in the Army of Nauvoo. They also condemn me for her sins."

"We're not here to make judgments," Martin said.

"If she has sinned," Ware replied, "so has Lael. If Amanda is excommunicated, Lael must suffer the same fate."

"Where is your daughter?" Traveler said.

"She was to be Lael's mission leader for the Army of Nauvoo. When Lael disappeared, Amanda came to me. I've kept her safe from her enemies and mine."

"We're working for the prophet," Traveler reminded him.

Ware stared at Traveler intently before reaching out and taking his hand. For a man known as a liberal, Ware still seemed to be believe in the old ways, like looking for devils by touch.

"Pray God he hasn't risen," Ware said. "Pray God you're not too late."

After giving them an address in Salt Lake, he dribbled away, attacking the basket with such ferocity that Traveler wished him luck chasing away the demons that haunted him.

25

Once back in Salt Lake, Traveler dropped his father at the genealogy library before going on to see Amanda Ware. Her apartment was at the end of a four-unit row house on First Avenue, not far from the Eagle Gate. The building had an unmistakable pioneer look, 1870s brickwork with crumbling buttresses and limestone bays.

The young woman met him on the narrow stoop despite the torrents of rain sluicing from the overhang. Looking at her, Traveler knew why the Army of Nauvoo had made her a missionary. She was petite, about five feet tall, and nonthreatening, with long blond hair and smiling blue eyes. Had he been ten years younger, he'd have joined up himself.

"My father called to tell me you were coming," she said, still smiling. "But I want to see some ID to be on the safe side."

When he handed her his wallet, she flipped through all the celluloid windows before returning it.

"Being named Moroni must be a burden for you," she said and motioned him inside.

The main room was bare except for a metal folding chair.

"My father owns this place," she said. "When he asked me

136

to stay here for a while, I agreed because it would serve as a reminder of what the Army of Nauvoo is fighting for. You see, it was built by a polygamist in the last century. Four houses in a row. Four wives. My father claims that's the reason he bought it, for the history. But you never can tell with men, even fathers."

Her smile faded. In that moment he knew she'd been using it as a mask to hide her fear.

"My father filled the cupboards with food and told me not to go out. Now you show up. Something's happened to Lael, hasn't it?"

Traveler tried reassuring her with a smile of his own. "Do you know where she is?"

"I should have known better than to let Lael join the Army of Nauvoo. I believe in our movement, but it's not for the likes of her."

Traveler walked around the room, pretending to examine the architecture while hoping his silence would prompt more information.

"Look at this place," she said. "Imagine what it must have been like for the women, lined up here in a row waiting for their lord and master to pick his partner for the night. It's a wonder they didn't murder him."

She pointed a finger at him. "A woman named Sojourner Truth, a black woman, was fighting for women back when Joe Smith and Brigham Young were enslaving us. 'Where did Christ come from?' she'd preach. 'From God and a woman. Man had nothing to do it.' "

She went to the window and stared out. "Do you think the rain will ever stop?"

"Tell me about Lael," Traveler said softly. "Please."

"What do you want to know?"

"Let's start with Reuben Kirkland."

Amanda sighed. "Lael and I were alone on the desk at army headquarters the day he walked in. Looking back on it, I think he'd come deliberately to meet Lael. At the time, of course, we thought it was our big chance to recruit a new member. We take men too, you know."

She settled onto the window's deep sill. "You should have seen Lael's eyes light up when he told us he was an atheist. She took it as a personal challenge to convert him to the church, or so she said later."

"Did you ever see him with anyone else?"

"Only that creep friend of his, Wayne Farley." She hugged herself. "The way he looked at me gave me the willies."

"What do you know about him?"

"Nothing really. He never said much, but he was always there, ready to do whatever Reuben told him."

"That's good to know," Traveler said. "Now tell me about the woman who gave you the thousand-dollar donation."

"How do you know about that?"

"Sarah Decker and I had a long talk."

"I've been trying to phone the general all day."

"Miz Decker told me she was going to visit relatives out of state," he said.

"I couldn't get hold of Jemma Hoyt either."

"I think she went along."

"It's bad, isn't it? Worse than I thought."

"The woman with the check," he reminded her.

Amanda shrugged. "Lael and I had gone on campus at BYU. We took Reuben with us too, against army regulations. Anyway, when I saw the amount of the check, I thought it was a joke."

"What did she look like, the woman who gave it to you?"

"Older. Maybe twenty-five or thirty. She was wearing a nice suit with a bag and matching shoes. Her clothes were expensive, like they'd come from Makoff's or someplace like that."

"What did she say?"

"Nothing. She just handed it over and walked away. That's what made me suspicious. Reuben too. He thought the check was a hoax just like I did, but not Lael. She said, 'If you work for what you believe in, God will step in and give you a hand.' That's when he kissed her."

Amanda flashed an on-off smile. "No one's ever kissed me like that."

"Do you know where I can find him?"

"He asked her to marry him, did you know that? Right there in front of me."

"What did Lael say?"

"What could she say? She told him he'd have to become a Saint and get his temple recommend so they could be bound together forever."

Traveler had heard the same thing from Claire once during one of her repentant, born-again moods. Even now, part of him still felt bound to her, and probably would while he lived, though the thought of dealing with her through eternity made him squirm.

"I know what you're thinking," Amanda said, "but you're wrong. Reuben didn't bat an eye. He kissed her again and said, 'All right, let's get me started on the way to sainthood.' After that, Lael couldn't wait to drop me off at army headquarters so they could go looking for a bishop to begin Roo's instruction."

Her eyes glistened. "Our mission never did get off the ground after that."

"Do you have any idea where they might be?"

"Do you know what they're saying about the weather?"

"Tell me."

"At church Sunday they read from Genesis instead of *The Book of Mormon.* 'And the water prevailed exceedingly upon the earth; and all the high hills, that were under the whole heaven, were covered. And all flesh died that moved upon the earth, both of fowl, and of cattle, and of beast, and of every creeping thing that creepeth upon the earth, and every man: All in whose nostrils was the breath of life, of all that was in the dry land, died.' " She turned to stare at him. "Do you think it's going to happen again?"

"I'm not a theologian."

"They say that our land of Zion is the ark now and that only the faithful will be saved. But Reuben isn't one of us. I don't think he means to be, either."

She shuddered. "I remember Lael saying, 'I'll take Roo to New Jerusalem one day, where we'll follow in the footsteps of Joseph Smith.' " Amanda wet her lips. "Maybe that's where they are now."

New Jerusalem, Traveler remembered from Sunday school, was in Missouri, where Joseph Smith said the land of Zion would be located one day along with the Mormons' Garden of Eden. Shortly after Smith's pronouncement, Missourians drove him and his followers out of their state.

"Do you know what Roo said to that?" she asked, then answered her own question. " 'You've got a deal. We'll go to Paradise together and find our own Eden.' "

26

Traveler sat in the Cherokee a long time trying to digest Amanda Ware's conversation. Even if he believed her every word, he didn't like what was happening. Paradise and Eden kept coming up in too many conversations, like deliberate road signs meant to guide him. But where exactly? To kidnappers, or along some convoluted path to salvation.

He snorted. Martin had taught him better than to think like that. *Find the girl*, Martin would say, *leave everything else to the church.*

Traveler checked his watch. There was an hour to go before he was scheduled to pick up his father at the genealogy library. That was more than enough time to wheedle a diagnosis out of old Dr. Murphy. Putting it to him was the problem. *Say, Doc, my father's been trying to phone the dead for the past week. What do you make of it? A touch of Alzheimer's or maybe a spot of senility?*

Groaning out loud, Traveler started the engine and headed higher on the avenues, where crossing State Street's Little Jordan was still possible.

Two blocks later, he'd come to a stop at the intersection of

Third Avenue and B Street when someone rear-ended him. A gray Plymouth filled his rearview mirror. Both its doors opened.

Traveler switched on the Jeep's emergency flashers and was about to get out when Stacie Breen tapped on the passenger-side window. Without thinking, he reached across the seat and unlocked the door. As soon as she opened it, her boy-friend, Jon, stepped out from behind her holding a gun.

"Shit," Traveler said.

Jon slid into the passenger seat. "Park behind Stacie."

"Point the gun somewhere else."

Grinning, the man cocked a cheap-looking revolver and stuck the muzzle against Traveler's ribs.

"Your size doesn't mean fuck against a thirty-eight," Jon said.

Traveler clenched his teeth and watched silently as Stacie returned to her Plymouth. She backed away from the Jeep and turned onto Third Avenue, heading downtown. Traveler followed. She parked half a block later. He pulled in right behind her.

She immediately abandoned the Plymouth for the Jeep's backseat. He watched in the mirror as she leaned forward to touch his shoulder.

"You hung up before I could say no," Traveler said. "I don't pay for information."

The .38 jabbed him.

"This is a nice car," Stacie said. "What do you think, Jon."

"Why not?"

She touched Traveler again. "You sign the registration over to us and I'll tell you where the boy is."

Traveler shook his head.

"Show him the picture," Jon said.

"I was getting to it."

Traveler heard her purse snap open.

"He looks just like you," she said, flicking his ear with a snapshot.

When he reached for it, Jon increased the muzzle pressure

142

against Traveler's side. Carefully, moving in slow motion, he grasped the photo and eased it into his field of vision. The focus was soft. The boy squinting into the sun looked like any other two-year-old.

"Cute, isn't he?" Stacie said.

"He isn't mine."

"Claire told me otherwise."

"We're wasting time." Jon began digging in the glove compartment with one hand while holding the .38 in the other. "Where's the goddamned registration?"

"This is my father's car," Traveler said.

"Bullshit. Look at this." He held up an insurance identification card. "It's in the name of Moroni Traveler."

"Senior," Traveler clarified. "I'm junior."

"Don't screw with me."

"That could be right," Stacie said. "Claire named the boy Moroni Traveler the third."

Jon shook his head. "Are you going to give us the car or not?"

"What the hell. The registration's in there somewhere. My father won't sue if I sign his name."

Jon shifted his body to get a better angle at the glove compartment. The .38 shifted too.

In one quick motion, Traveler rammed the web of his hand between the hammer and the firing pin and jerked the gun away. Jon's trigger finger snapped. His agonized cry sent Stacie fleeing into the rain. Only when Traveler failed to follow did she return to her Plymouth.

"You'd better straighten that finger before it swells," Traveler said.

Jon stopped panting long enough to say, "What the hell do you know?"

"I did worse than that playing football."

"You bastard," he said, cradling one hand in the other.

Traveler flipped open the cylinder and pretended to examine the cartridges. "Tell me where the boy is and you can walk away."

"I don't know, for God's sake."

Traveler shook his head.

"Stacie never told me." Jon blinked against the sweat running into his eyes. "She says that's her insurance policy."

"Where'd the snapshot come from?"

"She got it in the mail. That's all I know."

"Someone had to mail it."

Jon held up his misshapen finger, now the size of a knockwurst. "I gotta get to a doctor."

"That's just where I was headed. Do you want me to drive you?"

Sweat went flying as the man shook his head. Traveler reached across him to open the door.

"I'm good at finding people," Traveler said. "You remember that. Now get out."

"What do you want me to say to Stace?"

"Tell her we'll negotiate after she helps me find the boy."

"She'll kill me."

27

Dr. Wallace Murphy had his office in the Boston Building on Exchange Place. To get there, Traveler circled around to West Temple Street, avoiding the Little Jordan, turned east on Broadway, and then south on Main Street, which was running shoe-high at the moment.

He parked carefully, angling the Jeep Cherokee's front wheels against the curb and setting the emergency brake before fording Main Street. By the time he reached the Boston Building's wide granite steps, he was wet to the knees and feeling guilty about taking time out for personal business. Even so, he wanted a medical opinion about his father's erratic behavior.

A frieze of buffalo heads had formed a waterfall across the front of the building. Wondering what had happened to the pigeons that usually roosted on the stonework, Traveler plunged through the downpour and dripped across the marble lobby.

Memories of vaccinations and tongue depressors followed him into the elevator and up to Doc Murphy's office on the eighth floor. As usual, the waiting room was empty. Murphy hadn't taken on a new patient in years. Instead, he was retiring gradually, waiting for his longtimers to either die off or get tired of him.

A moment after Traveler rang the reception bell, the doctor slid back the frosted glass panel himself. "Moroni. Lucky you caught me. I was about to close up shop and go home before they close down Main Street."

Murphy shut the panel and opened the connecting door that led to his office on the left and his examination room to the right. Traveler turned left.

"I take it you're not sick," Murphy said, slipping behind his desk which was cluttered with medical journals. He was dressed the same as always: gray herringbone sport coat, charcoal slacks, and oxblood loafers.

"It's Martin," Traveler said.

Murphy sighed. "I'd be a rich man if I had a dollar for every time you or your father had said that about the other."

Traveler sank into the patient's chair. "Martin tried to phone his father."

The doctor pursed his lips. Wrinkles spread from his brow across the top of his bald head.

"His grandfather, too," Traveler added. "He's suddenly obsessed with the dead."

"Is that all? In this town, that's normal behavior."

"Not for Martin."

"I know all about it. It's this new lady of his, Jolene Clawson. She's a part-time researcher at the genealogy library and a patient of mine for the last twenty years. Hell, I introduced them when Martin asked me if I knew anybody who could research family trees."

"When was this?"

"A month ago, maybe a little less. Just last week he called and thanked me for putting him on to her. He said he'd hired her to write your family history."

"I've been asking him about it for years," Traveler said.

"I'll tell you what I told Martin. Some things are best left to memory."

"What did he say to that?"

Murphy shrugged. "That he was going to have it bound in red leather."

"Martin was in the army when I was born," Traveler said. The doctor steepled his fingers but said nothing.

"He'd been away nearly two years."

"Your mother was my patient, too. I can't betray her trust."

"You signed the birth certificate listing Martin as my father."

Murphy stood up and came around the desk. "I think we'd both better leave before the water gets any higher."

28

Traveler called the genealogy library and was quickly connected with his father.

"Jolene's here," Martin said the moment he came on the line.

"Does that mean you can't talk?"

"Hell, no. We've been hard at work. We may have saved your ass."

"Watch your language," Jolene said in the background.

"Women," Martin said. "Speaking of which, guess who Lael's stepmother is." He snorted and went on without waiting for Traveler's response. "Crystal Moseby was her maiden name, daughter of the First Apostle. Think about it."

Traveler did. Seth Woolley, Elton Woolley's nephew and his closest living relative, had divorced his first wife to marry the daughter of the man rumored to be next in line to become God's living prophet.

Martin lowered his voice. "I think maybe I ought to look a little further. What with Utah's history of polygamy, who knows what might turn up. We could all be related to Moseby. Anyway, we'll be burning the midnight oil here."

"Are you trying to tell me something?" Traveler asked.

"Your mother never knew him, if that's what you mean."

"I talked to Doctor Murphy," Traveler said.

"Are you sick?"

"I was checking up on you."

"Where the hell are you?"

"The Boston Building."

"You'd better go over to the office and find Newel Ellsworth. He called in a couple of hours ago and said he had to talk to you."

Traveler glanced toward the entrance. Outside, a pair of workmen were erecting a temporary awning to divert the runoff away from the front steps. "Did he say why?"

"All he said was, 'Tell Moroni I'm coming in out of the wilderness.' "

The Chester Building was four blocks away, but Traveler had to detour more than a mile to reach it. By the time he did, police had the street closed. At first he figured the floodwaters were threatening the temple. Then he saw the ambulance parked in front of the Chester Building, with a stretcher about to be loaded on board.

He stopped the truck right where it was, nose to nose with a barricading patrol car, and sprinted for the ambulance. A policeman gave chase. Traveler was about to be arrested when Willis Tanner pushed through the Chester Building's bronze door and waved away the officer.

"What's wrong?" Traveler panted.

"Newel Ellsworth's been killed."

Before Traveler could respond, the ambulance pulled away from the curb.

"Let's get under cover," Tanner said. "I don't want to attract a crowd."

Traveler allowed himself to be herded inside. Two uniformed policemen were there ahead of him, as was Anson Horne, a lieutenant specializing in police-church liaison. His goal in life, he'd once bragged, was to arrest Moroni Traveler and Son for misuse of an angel's name.

Horne pointed a finger at Traveler and pretended to shoot him. His other hand held a small two-way radio.

"Not a word about the girl," Tanner whispered in Traveler's ear.

"We've arrested some friends of yours," Horne said, blowing on his finger.

Traveler pushed past the lieutenant and headed for the cigar stand. The eternal flame was out and Nephi Bates was behind the counter.

"The blasphemers have been brought to justice," Bates said.

"He means Bill and Charlie," Tanner said.

Traveler half-turned to see that Horne had followed him, though the uniformed officers had stayed behind guarding the door.

"Where's Barney?" Traveler asked.

Horne grinned. "He's out trying to raise bail, assuming we allow it."

"Would you mind telling me what happened?"

Rather than look up, the policeman aimed his words at Traveler's collarbone. "Your buddy, Newel Ellsworth, was shot on the sidewalk out front. Someone walked right up to him, put a gun against his chest, and pulled the trigger."

Traveler stared at Tanner. "Come on, Willis. You can't believe Bill and Charlie did something like that."

"They're not charged with murder," Horne said.

"What the hell are you up to?"

"Easy, Mo." Tanner squinted to camouflage his tic. "They started yelling about some kind of church conspiracy. We had to get them off the street."

Horne chuckled. "I've charged them with arson."

"The house in Magna, the one the Sisters Cumorah rented, burned down," Tanner explained. "We're still investigating."

"Yeah," Horne added, "maybe we'll put it down to vandalism if you do as you're told."

"What does Bill say?"

"He's asking for a lawyer," Tanner said.

Traveler paced to the elevator and back, reminding himself to stay calm. "Ellsworth was working for me."

"Doing what?" Horne demanded.

"He needed the money. I didn't expect him to come up with anything."

"About what?"

"The devil." Traveler glanced at Tanner. "Willis here can tell you more about that subject."

"God help us," Bates said from behind the cigar counter. "The devil has risen."

"Lieutenant," Tanner said, "I think we'd better talk."

Without waiting for Horne's reply, Tanner put his arm around the policeman's shoulder and walked him as far as the revolving door. While they whispered, Horne kept his glare focused on Traveler. Finally, the policeman shook his head and shouted, "It's on your head."

Tanner said something Traveler couldn't hear.

The policeman shrugged, gave his hand-held two-way radio to Tanner, and then signaled his men to follow him outside.

When Tanner returned to the cigar counter, he nodded at Bates. "I think you'd better take the elevator up top and check for leaks."

Bates raised his hand, almost a salute, before trotting to the elevator. As soon as he disappeared, Tanner shook his head. "You shouldn't have mentioned the devil, Moroni."

"Jesus, Willis. Use your head. Newel didn't get himself killed over graffiti or some damned rumor. He must have found out something about the girl."

Tanner's mouth opened but nothing came out.

"Considering your promises of secrecy," Traveler said, "a lot of people seem to know about the kidnapping."

Static hissed from the radio in Tanner's hand. At the same time, he glanced toward the empty grillwork cage to make sure the elevator hadn't returned.

Traveler said, "How many people know what's really going on?"

"The prophet and the apostles. That's it."

Traveler thought that over. If Elton Woolley had told Ware, he might have told someone else. "Don't lie to me now, Willis. It could have been Bill or Charlie who was shot, or even my father."

"Then the sooner you find Lael, the better."

"Call Horne back in here and put him to work. Better yet, call in the FBI, because time is running out and you're going to need some help finding her."

Before Tanner had time to reply, cables clattered inside the elevator shaft. A moment later, Nephi Bates arrived on the ground floor, opened the accordion door, and took tentative steps toward the cigar stand.

"I'm out of it," Traveler said. "Favor or no favor, I don't take chances when it comes to my father."

Tanner's tic forced him to close one eye as he raised the radio to his mouth. "Lieutenant Horne, can you hear me?"

"Go ahead," the policeman said.

"I want Mad Bill and the Indian arrested on suspicion of murder."

"Yes, sir."

"You bastard," Traveler said. Out of the corner of his eyes, he saw Bates slip behind the counter.

"And, Lieutenant," Tanner added, "don't charge them formally until you hear from me."

"What about Traveler? Do you want me to arrest him too?"

"Stay away from him. That's an order."

"Roger."

Tanner slipped the radio into the pocket of his raincoat. "I'm sure the prophet will rest easier, Mo, knowing you have more incentive than ever."

Traveler grabbed Tanner's lapels and shook him. Bates gasped but made no move to intervene.

"Go ahead, Mo. Do what you have to, just as I will when it comes to protecting the prophet."

Traveler released his hold. "If you're trying to make me feel guilty, it won't work."

"To be near the prophet and the spoken word of our Father should be enough for any man," Tanner said. "But I'm your friend, too. I'm protecting your interests."

"We've known each other a long time, Willis, long enough for me to know that you probably believe that. Hell. I guess I believe you, too, for what it's worth."

Traveler started for the door.

"Where are you going, Moroni?"

"You said it yourself. We must look to our fathers."

Tanner ran after him. "Wait up, Mo, I apologize. I'm just trying to do my job. I . . . look outside. The rain is letting up. I'm sure of it."

"Hallelujah!" Bates shouted.

29

Lael's father, Seth Woolley, lived high up on South Temple Street, well past the governor's mansion but still among the gentry. Traveler guessed the house to be turn of the century, Greek Revival in style, though he preferred to think of it as scaled-down *Gone With the Wind*. The front door, crowned by an arched window of beveled glass, was opened by Woolley himself.

The man scowled and said, "If you don't mind, we'll talk out here, under the portico."

"You should put a sign up," Traveler said. "No Gentiles allowed." He stepped past Woolley and into a vestibule that opened onto a massive staircase worthy of Scarlett O'Hara.

Woolley fanned the door, reluctant to close it. "It's blasphemy to have a man like you named for our angel."

"Don't be fooled by the change in weather." Traveler pointed out a break in the cloud cover. "I figure the devil's still at work out there somewhere."

Woolley slammed the door. "If you haven't brought my daughter home, why are you here?"

"People who withhold information shouldn't expect miracles."

"Are you calling me a liar?" Woolley said.

"Why didn't you tell me you'd divorced Lael's mother to marry the First Apostle's daughter?"

"That has nothing to do with Lael being missing."

"There are a lot of people in this land of Zion who might misunderstand your attitude. Even the prophet himself might start thinking that a man like yourself, a man with a new young wife, could turn his back on the past in expectation of future children."

"You . . . heathen." Woolley clenched his fists so hard they shook. "If you weren't working for my uncle, I'd throw you out of here."

Instead of replying, Traveler crossed the vestibule to an open door. Lights were on in the room beyond, a walnut-paneled library. Built-in bookcases, filled with leather-bound volumes, took up every inch of wall space except for a pair of leaded-pane windows. The books looked as if they'd been arranged by size and color.

A desk half the size of Traveler's office stood at one end of the room. Traveler moved behind it before Woolley had the chance.

"What is it you want from me?" Woolley said.

Traveler waved him toward the only chair, a ladder-back on the other side of the room. Woolley raised his fists. For a moment, Traveler thought the man was going to put up a fight. Then suddenly he relaxed his hands and sighed. His shoulders sagged and his head hung as he dragged the chair across an Oriental rug to sit as supplicant in front of the desk.

Traveler nodded at a framed wedding picture in front of him. "What did the prophet say when you divorced Lael's mother?"

"Being related to a man like Elton Woolley isn't easy. Sometimes I feel as if I'd spent my entire life trying to live up to him." He shook his head slowly. "As a child, people kept expecting things from me. Insight! Revelations. I don't know. Uncle Elton was no different. I could never satisfy him."

"Being related didn't stop you from shedding your wife, did it?"

Woolley shrugged.

"With your uncle as sick as he is, maybe dying," Traveler said, "it occurs to me that marrying Elihu Moseby's daughter was a smart move on your part, especially if he becomes the next prophet."

"You don't know anything about my life."

"Then tell me about it."

He stared at Traveler for a while before continuing. "You try to be worthy, but no matter what you do it's not enough. People look at you and shake their heads. But what happens when they don't look at you anymore, when the prophet is gone and you're no better than anyone else?"

"You tell me."

Woolley reached for the wedding photograph. "It's not the way you think. I love Crystal."

Traveler stayed the man's hand. "I have the feeling I've seen her before."

"Of course you have. But you have to understand. It's not like a regular job for Crystal. My wife doesn't get paid. A man in my position, a bishop of the church, couldn't allow that. Earning our daily bread isn't woman's work."

Recognition caused Traveler to release the photo. She was more than the First Apostle's daughter, she was his driver.

"You condemn me like everyone else," Woolley went on. "But what could I do when a man like Moseby asks my permission? 'I feel safe with Chris,' he says. 'I trust her. Allow an old man the luxury of his daughter's company for a while at least, until the children come.' "

Woolley leaned back and closed his eyes. "It's like everything else in my life. It wasn't a request. It was a command. 'My Chris,' he calls her. 'As close to me as any son could be.' I prayed for insight, for the enlightenment that everyone expected from me. I failed as always, just like I've done with my daughter over the years." He opened his eyes. "Crystal should be home, cooking meals, taking care of the house. My friends are laughing at me behind my back. I know it."

"It's dinnertime now," Traveler said.

"I never know when she'll be home."

"I was hoping to talk to her."

"You'd better get Moseby's permission for that."

"I could wait for her here."

With a shrug, Woolley returned the silver frame to its place on the desk. Traveler studied the photograph more carefully. In it, Seth Woolley looked old enough to be father of the bride.

"I asked Lael to be a bridesmaid," Woolley said. "But I should have known better. She and Crystal never got along. That first time they met, Crystal said, 'We must listen to our fathers and follow their footsteps.' Lael's answer to that was to join the Army of Nauvoo. 'One of us,' she told me, 'has to bring enlightenment to women.' 'What about the man you've taken up with?' my wife said. 'He's an atheist waiting to be saved,' my daughter answered."

"Why didn't you tell me this before?" Traveler said.

"My first wife used to say that Lael was born to compensate for me."

"What did she mean by that?"

Woolley shook his head. "Lael's a deep one, like her uncle. You'll probably think I'm crazy, but there've been times when I thought my daughter could look inside my head and read my thoughts. You've never met her, have you?"

"No," Traveler said.

"You'll understand when you do. She has the prophet's eyes, you know."

"The atheist you mentioned, is that Reuben Kirkland?"

"If she comes to harm, people will blame me for that. They'll say I should have raised her better. Even the prophet condemns me. I've seen it in his face."

Woolley pounded his knees with his fists. "My daughter told me once that she had a dream, a vision, and in it an angel told her she must save a soul before she dies. 'Otherwise,' Lael said, 'my lifetime here on earth will be wasted.' Do you think that Kirkland's soul was meant to make amends for me?"

"Where can I find your wife?"

Woolley sighed. "You find the First Apostle and you'll find her."

"Do you have any suggestions where I should look at this moment?" Traveler said.

"The last I heard from my wife, her father was keeping the genealogy library open all night for *you*. Obviously that wasn't true, since you're here."

"Do you remember her exact words?"

He shrugged. "That you, Moroni Traveler, had some important research to do."

"My father's named Moroni, too," Traveler said. "When he chooses to use it."

30

Stars were showing as Traveler drove down South Temple Street. The radio was reporting that a second storm was stalled in the California Sierras, dropping snow on Donner Pass. If it continued to stay there, forecasters were predicting a thirty percent chance that the new front would run out of steam completely by the time it crossed Nevada into Utah. Behind that storm, the announcer said, were blue skies all the way to Hawaii.

Despite the break in the weather, runoff from City Creek still had State Street barricaded with sandbags. Traveler detoured to higher ground before reaching the genealogy library on North Temple.

He parked his father's Jeep out front, the only vehicle on the street. By the time he got out of the Cherokee, two men were waiting for him, obviously church security. One of them knew Traveler by sight. They both escorted him inside and turned him over to a librarian whose plastic name tag read *Mrs. Christensen.* She eyed her watch pointedly before ushering him through a maze of computer terminals to a cubbyhole where Martin and Jolene were at work.

"Take a seat," Martin said. "We'll talk to our ancestors."

"Now, Moroni," Jolene said. "Remember where you are."

Traveler grinned. Few people got away with calling his father Moroni.

Jolene Clawson was sixty or so, a thin, busty woman with gray hair bleached white. She was, Martin had once said, what Kary might have looked like had she lived long enough.

"I was told that Elihu Moseby was here," Traveler said.

"You don't see him, do you?" Martin replied.

"The First Apostle has been very helpful," Jolene said. "We have him to thank for Sister Christensen here. She's a senior librarian."

The woman forced a smile before retreating to her desk, which was out of earshot but still within easy striking distance.

Martin left his chair to kiss Jolene on the cheek. "My son and I have family business."

"Fine by me, but you watch your language in here." She kissed him back, an airy peck, before vacating her chair to join Mrs. Christensen.

Martin patted the empty chair. As soon as Traveler sat down his father turned back to the computer terminal and typed in a request.

A listing for Ned Payson, Traveler's grandfather on his mother's side of the family, came on the screen.

"Wouldn't you know Kary's kin would be a dentist," Martin said. "No empathy in that bloodline."

"You sent me to him as a child."

"You know your mother. What choice did I have?"

Traveler clenched his teeth, remembering the ethyl chloride Ned used instead of novocaine. *It won't hurt,* Ned lied every time.

Martin hit another key. Ned's family tree grew.

"Let's see your side of the family," Traveler said.

With a keystroke, his father turned the screen blank. "We haven't got time to waste. Now let me explain how this works. For decades the church has been sending out missionaries to collect damn near every record in the world. Marriage certificates, birth certificates, death certificates. They've walked cemeteries everywhere, recording tombstones, seeking the dead just as Joe Smith decreed. It's all here, at our fingertips."

"Try Moseby," Traveler said.

"Why?"

"Because I don't want any more surprises, like finding out Moseby's daughter is also his driver."

Nodding, Martin typed in MOSEBY, ELIHU.

The terminal beeped.

RESTRICTED FILE blinked on the screen. ACCESS DENIED.

"Shit!" Martin murmured.

Traveler glanced toward Mrs. Christensen's desk. "Try again."

More beeps.

"Damn," Martin said.

Traveler checked the librarian again. This time two security men were blocking his view.

The biggest one, armed with a nightstick, said, "Sorry, gentlemen. You'll have to leave." The second man carried a two-way radio in one hand.

Martin ignored them to type in Moseby's name again. This time the beep persisted.

"Use your heads," Martin said, "We're here at this time of night because the First Apostle opened the library for us."

"Requesting backup," the smaller man said into his radio.

Jolene and Mrs. Christensen stepped out from behind the guards.

"It's true, I'm here at the apostle's request," Mrs. Christensen said, "but he didn't say anything about giving you people access to restricted files." She stared at the computer screen. "Access denied means just that."

Traveler heard the sound of running feet. A moment later two more security men arrived. These two were armed.

"Don't get excited," Traveler said. "There's a letter I want to show you. My inside coat pocket." Very slowly, he reached for the plastic bag that contained Elton Woolley's carte blanche.

Once unwrapped, he handed the document to Mrs. Christensen, who grasped it by her fingertips as if fearing contamination. As soon as she looked at it, her face reddened, her hand trembled.

"The prophet has spoken," she whispered, holding the letter at arm's length so the security men could read it.

They watched with awe as Traveler rewrapped the letter and tucked it away.

"What we're doing here is confidential," he said. "Mrs. Christensen may stay because we need her help with the computer."

The guards nodded and hurried away, looking relieved. Once they were gone, the librarian supplied the access code.

The moment Martin typed it into the computer, the screen filled with data. Elihu Moseby, like all good Saints, had been fruitful and multiplied. He had three sons, Elihu Jr., Malachi, and Orson, and four daughters, Emerald, Ruby, Beryl, and Crystal. His wife, Anna, née Rockwell, came from the well-known pioneer family that gave its name to a chain of clothing stores, Rockwell's, with branches in Salt Lake, Provo, Ogden, and Cedar City.

"Look at the daughters," Traveler told his father. "Every one a gemstone."

"I'll be damned." Martin keyed in the name Opal Taylor.

Nothing came up. He tried again with the same result. Mrs. Christensen took his place at the computer. After twenty minutes of repeated failures, she sat back and scowled at the computer screen. "I don't understand it. Taylor is a prominent name. Who is she?"

"The head of a local women's group," Martin said.

"Then we should have a listing for her."

"Are there any other restricted access codes?" Traveler asked.

"None that I'm aware of."

"Maybe Opal Taylor has been erased," Martin said.

Mrs. Christensen shook her head emphatically. "That's a

162

possibility, of course. But Taylor's an English name. We have every record available from that country. If Opal Taylor's not in our computer, it's my opinion that no one by that name ever existed."

31

Traveler waited for morning before driving to the state capitol.
The building stood at the top of State Street, overlooking the
entire Salt Lake valley. For the first time in a week, the skies
were blue and the headwaters of the Little Jordan were no
more than a trickle.

The building, constructed of Utah granite like the temple,
was a small-scale version of the national capitol, domed in the
center with two wings, one for each branch of the legislature.
In theory there was total separation of church and state in
Utah. In practice Traveler had no trouble finding a civil servant
who would honor Elton Woolley's carte blanche.

An hour later, armed with a complete records check on
Opal Taylor, Traveler returned to the Chester Building to consult his father. Martin was on the phone doing his best to
reassure Willis Tanner.

"Moroni left first thing this morning, Willis." Martin held up
crossed fingers to alleviate the lie. "No, he didn't say where he
was going, but I'm sure he's on the job."

Martin waved to ask Traveler if he wanted his presence
known. Traveler nodded that he did and sat down in the
sunlight flooding his desk.

"You're in luck," Martin said into the phone. "He just came
through the door."

Traveler picked up his extension. "I need to meet with the First Apostle."

"What's happened?" Tanner asked.

"This morning if possible."

Tanner caught his breath but ignored the rebuff. "He's got a heavy schedule today, so I'm manning the command center. If there's something you need, I'll take care of it."

"I want his driver there, too," Traveler said. "Or should I say daughter."

"You've come up with something, haven't you? I can hear it in your voice."

"Willis!"

"All right. I'll talk to him and get back to you as soon as I can."

The moment Tanner hung up, Traveler swung his chair around to face the temple. At the top of one spire, the Angel Moroni's statue looked close enough to touch.

Martin rolled his chair over to join Traveler at the window.

"They're calling the change in weather a miracle," Martin said.

Bright sunlight made the temple granite shine like white marble.

"They say another day of rain would have destroyed the land of Zion."

Traveler grunted. "Who does?"

"Bill and Charlie, of course. I talked to them in jail this morning."

"What about bail?"

"I'm afraid we'll need a lawyer if we're going to get anywhere."

Traveler leaned forward until his head touched the glass. To the west, beyond the Great Salt Lake, a line of dark clouds blurred the horizon. "It looks like the new storm front got past the Sierras after all."

"Bill says—"

The phone rang.

Traveler spun around to grab the receiver. "Willis, I—"

"It's me, Moroni. Stacie Breen."

In that moment before she identified herself, he'd thought it was Claire back from the dead.

"I called to give you one last chance."

Claire used to say the same thing.

"Are you listening?"

"Yes." Traveler motioned his father to pick up the extension on his desk.

"Moroni Traveler the Third needs a father," she said.

For his father's benefit Traveler asked, "How much do you want this time?"

"Claire told me that with you it was a matter of motivation. She said you wouldn't come to her rescue unless you thought she was in trouble."

"She cried wolf once too often," Martin put in. "It got her killed."

"Who else is on the line?" she demanded.

"Moroni Traveler the First," Martin answered.

"That's all right then."

"Get to the point," Traveler said.

"I could tell you the boy's in danger, but then I'm not Claire. You don't love *me*."

Martin made a face and mouthed, "Women."

"I've decided to hold an auction," Stacie went on. "I'll sell the boy to the highest bidder."

"Are you talking about the boy in person or just his location?"

She snorted. "That's for you to worry about."

"You're bluffing just like Claire," Martin said. "You've only got two buyers, us."

"People are standing in line to adopt children."

"When and where is the auction?" Traveler asked.

"Now that I'm sure you're interested, I'll let you know."

She hung up laughing at him, something Claire had done often enough.

As soon as Traveler replaced the receiver, the phone rang again. "Ten minutes," Tanner said. "The Hotel Utah roof garden."

32

The Hotel Utah, with its enameled white brick facade, glazed terra-cotta scrollwork, and ornate beehive cupola, was once the finest hotel in the West. Its roof garden restaurant had been a yearly birthday treat when Traveler was growing up.

Now it was a church office building, with enough security checkpoints to get Traveler searched twice before he reached the elevators. From there, he was escorted all the way to the roof, where he was turned over to Crystal Woolley.

The First Apostle was seated at a white metal table overlooking the temple across the street. In the center of the table, a golden beehive-shaped tray held a pitcher of lemonade and three crystal tumblers. Sunlight reflecting through the glass prisms covered the tabletop with rainbows.

Moseby rose, buttoning his blue blazer before shaking hands. "Congratulations. I understand from Willis that you're making progress."

"That's his assumption."

"Well now. You'd better sit down and explain that. Chris, pour Mr. Traveler a glass of lemonade."

She carefully measured out three glasses, then took hers far enough away to be out of earshot.

Traveler sipped. The lemonade was too sweet for his taste. "I want to thank you for opening the genealogy library for my father last night."

"Of course," Moseby said. "They tell me you looked up my family history." He shrugged. "Boring stuff, so that can't be why you're here."

"Emerald, Beryl, Ruby, and Crystal." Traveler smiled. "Gemstones as in Opal. Opal Taylor."

"Now that you mention it, I like the name. I should have given it to my daughter, Ruby, who's always complaining that Ruby sounds ethnic."

Moseby removed his glasses and polished them on an immaculately ironed white handkerchief before continuing. "But that's not what you're asking, is it? You're thinking that maybe I have some connection with this Taylor woman. I assure you, however, that I don't know anybody by that name."

"Neither do the church computers."

"So I've heard from our librarians. Of course, there may be bugs in our genealogy system. I'm no expert on software and the like. But the fact that she's not listed with us doesn't mean she won't show up somewhere else."

"Exactly my thinking." Traveler took another sip of his lemonade. "That's why I ran her name through a records check at the state capitol."

Moseby topped off Traveler's glass. "How did you manage that?"

"I had help from the prophet."

Judging from Moseby's blank look, the First Apostle hadn't been told about the carte blanche.

"The state computers came up with only one Opal Taylor. She died in 1934."

Traveler glanced at Moseby's daughter, who was standing at the parapet staring across Main Street at the temple.

"When I checked out that license plate number you ran for me," Traveler said "I didn't come up with Opal Taylor. The name I got was Reuben Kirkland."

"Someone's going to pay for giving me bad information.

Moseby pounded the table so hard the crystal pitcher fell over, shattering. His daughter whirled around, but he motioned her to stay where she was.

Traveler said, "In case you've forgotten, I was talking to you on the phone when you had Willis Tanner type that license plate number into your computer. The bad information came from you."

"Chris!" Moseby shouted. "Get me Willis Tanner on the phone. Now."

"Don't bother," Traveler said. "I don't want to put him in the middle."

"Suit yourself." Moseby rose from the table. "Chris, you'd better find a broom and clean up this mess."

Traveler stayed seated. "If we can believe that genealogy computer of yours, you married into a very prominent family, the Rockwells. I bought my first suit from Rockwell Clothiers, a blue double-breasted for my high school prom."

Grudgingly, the First Apostle eased back into his chair. His daughter stood behind him. Her sharply pointed shoes made Traveler wonder if she'd been one of the women who'd way-laid him.

Traveler smiled. "If I remember my history, the Rockwells started out as tailors. That's spelled differently, of course, t-a-i-l-o-r instead of T-a-y-l-o-r. But I think you can see what I'm getting at."

"A coincidence of names isn't proof of anything."

"What do you think a man like Elton Woolley would say about it?"

"He's not talking to anyone at the moment. Maybe he never will again. Besides, what's the word of a Gentile like yourself against the church's First Apostle? If I were you, Mr. Traveler, I'd look to *The Book of Mormon*. 'He that fighteth against Zion, both Jew and Gentile, both bond and free, both male and female, shall perish; for they who are not for me are against me, saith our God.' "

33

Traveler headed for the Chester Building to consult his *Book of Mormon*. Two men followed him from the Hotel Utah. They both wore raincoats despite the sunshine. Traveler had more faith; he'd left his coat in the car.

The moment he entered the office, his father turned away from the window and said, "You're being followed."

"I know. Two men in raincoats."

"I make it three."

Traveler looked for himself. Number three had been walking by the hotel when Traveler came out. There'd been no sign of his raincoat at the time.

Martin pointed toward the west, where the clouds on the horizon had grown into thunderheads. "The look on your face tells me we're in for more than rain."

"Sit down," Traveler said, "and listen to this."

For the next few minutes, he replayed his interview with the First Apostle. When he finished, Martin went back to staring out the window.

"Those must be Moseby's men out there."

Traveler nodded. "He's been playing games with us from the beginning."

"What the hell do we do about it?"

"According to the Ware girl, Lael Woolley used to preach to her boyfriend, Reuben Kirkland. Something about taking him to New Jerusalem one day to show him where the city of Zion would be built."

Traveler began rummaging in his desk. "Where's our *Book of Mormon?*"

Martin patted his coat before bringing out their pocket-size edition. "Before you got here, I was refreshing my memory on baptisms for the dead."

He slipped behind his desk and began thumbing through the book's index. "Here's what we want. Doctrine and Covenants. 'Hearken, O ye elders of my church, saith the Lord your God, who have assembled yourselves together, according to my commandments, in this land, which is the land of Missouri, which is the land I have appointed and consecrated for the gathering of the saints. Wherefore, this is the land of promise, and the place for the city of Zion.' That's Joe Smith speaking, back in 1831. The church has been buying up Jackson County, Missouri, where he said the Garden of Eden was located, ever since."

"I'm a dummy," Traveler said. "I was on my way to the town of New Eden when Moseby had me called back. Supposedly, the Sisters Cumorah and the nonexistent Opal Taylor were threatening to make the kidnapping public."

"If you're saying Moseby's behind it, it doesn't make sense. He has nothing to gain by kidnapping the girl or from a false revelation either, for that matter."

Traveler said, "What about Newel Ellsworth? Why kill him?"

Martin shook his head. "New Eden's a long way to drive if it starts to rain. It would be easier to call Willis and have him check it out."

"He can't afford to cross someone like Elihu Moseby."

34

Despite gathering thunderheads along the western skyline, good weather held all the way to Hyrum. But when Traveler and his father turned north, a squall line descended from the Wasatch Mountains, slowing their progress. As a result, they didn't reach New Eden, population 1,692, until dusk.

They cruised the length of Main Street before backtracking to park in front of the Tithing Office. Lights were on in half a dozen buildings along the two blocks that made up the town's business district.

Traveler opened the glove box, took out the .45, and slipped it into his pocket.

"Jesus Christ," Martin whispered, a prayer. "I hope you don't have to use that."

Together, they climbed out of the Jeep and headed for the squat, rock-faced building across the street. A sheet metal sign hanging from brackets above the door squeaked in the wind. HANSEN'S DRY GOODS, NILES HANSEN, PROPRIETOR AND SHERIFF.

The man behind the counter was wearing a heavy flannel shirt and Levi's new enough to have come off one of his own table displays. He was Martin's height, five-six, bald-headed, and somewhere in his fifties. He took one look at Traveler and said, "If you're looking for the sheriff, that's me, Niles Hansen."

Traveler and his father introduced themselves and handed over their IDs.

"I don't do much real police work around here," Sheriff Hansen said after checking their credentials. "We're not like Salt Lake yet, thank God."

"We're looking for a young woman," Traveler said.

"A runaway?"

"Her name's Lael Woolley."

"Not *the* Woolley?"

Martin nodded. "The prophet's grandniece."

The sheriff shook his head emphatically. "I'd know if she was around here."

"What about the motel up the street?" Traveler asked.

"That's our one and only, the Garden of Eden. The last time I talked to Scott Miller, its owner, only two cabins were rented. What with the weather we've been having, he's lucky to have anyone staying there."

The sheriff hit himself on the forehead with the heel of his hand. "Son of a bitch, pardon my French, but there's a honeymoon couple staying up there. Is that what this is about, an elopement?"

Traveler unwrapped Lael's photograph and handed it to the sheriff.

"You know how it is with honeymooners." Hansen rubbed his bald head and grinned. "They never come out of their room." He returned the photo.

"Does this man Miller have a phone?" Traveler asked.

"We're not that far out in the sticks. Before I call him, though, I want to know what's going on."

Martin shook his head. "The Woolley name ought to be enough to get your cooperation."

The sheriff smiled. "The trouble is, I've only got your word for it so far."

"This ought to help." Traveler gave him the prophet's carte blanche.

Hansen swallowed so hard his Adam's apple shimmied. "Jesus, pardon my French again, just tell me what you want."

"Call the motel, but be careful." Traveler moved to the wall phone behind the counter so he could listen in. "If we're right, the girl is being held against her will."

"My God, kidnapping."

Traveler handed him the receiver.

The sheriff took a deep breath and dialed. "Scott, is that you?"

"Who else would it be, Niles?"

"Are you alone?"

"What's going on?"

"Are you alone?"

"Just like always."

"That honeymoon couple you've got there. I want you to describe the girl."

"You're turning into a dirty old man."

"Just do it."

The motel owner sighed. "Dark hair, light skin. Maybe twenty, twenty-one. Pretty in a thin sort of way."

"What about her eyes?" Traveler mouthed into the sheriff's ear, who passed on the question.

"You'd remember them if you saw her," the motel man said. "Big dark eyes, eyes that eat you up."

"That's her," Traveler whispered.

"They've got a friend with them," the man added. "He's in the cabin next to theirs."

"Listen to me, Scott. Don't say a thing about this call."

"You still haven't told me what it's all about."

Using both hands, Traveler made a beckoning motion.

"On second thought," the sheriff translated, "I want you to get down here as fast as you can. Now."

"I'm on my way."

The sheriff hung up. "What now?"

Traveler didn't want anyone overreacting, especially the

174

local law. On the other hand, backup was always a good idea. "We ought to have some help," he said.

"I've got one volunteer deputy, Marv Hatch."

"You'd better call him."

"You're damn right," Martin said. "We'll need the two of you covering the back of the motel."

The sheriff rubbed his forehead hard enough to redden the skin. "You think there's going to be trouble?"

"That's what we're trying to avoid."

"I'll never get Marv on the phone. He sleeps like a hibernating bear. I'll have to go get him myself. It shouldn't take more than ten minutes. When Miller gets here from the motel, make sure he stays put."

The sheriff's deputy had come out of hibernation with cowlicked hair, rumpled clothes, and a 12-gauge pump shotgun that was pointed at Traveler's chest.

"It's just like you wanted," the sheriff said. "Marv here is my backup. He's going to make sure we all stay put until more help arrives."

"What kind of help?" Martin asked.

Hansen tapped the side of his head. "You didn't expect me to take a letter like that on face value, did you? Anyone could forge the prophet's signature."

"Who the hell did you call?"

"It took me a while, but I finally got through to church headquarters in Salt Lake. They said help was already on the way."

"How did they know you needed help?" Traveler asked.

"They didn't say."

"What did they say about my letter?"

"I talked to a man named Tanner. He said I could trust you, but not to make a move until the troops got here."

"I don't like the sound of that," Martin said.

The sheriff checked his watch. "Thank God the rain's held off, because just about now my counterpart in Hyrum is turning on the lights at the high school football field so the helicopters can land. Once they do, he'll convoy the bunch of them over here."

Twenty minutes later, Elihu Moseby walked into Hansen's Dry Goods. He was dressed in a hunting jacket, fatigue pants, and army boots. With him were a dozen men carrying automatic rifles and wearing flak jackets. Their heads were covered with black baseball hats embroidered with golden beehives.

Martin shook his head in despair. Traveler knew how he felt. No uniforms meant church security, maybe even Danites.

Sheriff Hansen described the situation at the Garden of Eden Motel. The honeymooners, registered as Mr. and Mrs. Reuben Kirkland, were in one cabin, their friend, Wayne Farley, in the adjoining unit, which had a connecting door.

"What do you know about the friend?" Moseby asked.

"Just what our motel man tells me. He's big and rough-looking."

Moseby turned to his troops. "You all know what to do. Your team leader will move you into position. Wait for my signal."

Silently, the troops filed out in the night.

Traveler waited for the door to close behind them before asking, "What are we supposed to do?"

With a jerk of his head, Moseby sent the sheriff outside.

"Willis Tanner is at the hospital waiting for your call." He handed Traveler a paper with a telephone number on it. "He's with the prophet."

Tanner sounded jubilant when he came on the line. "Elton sends his congratulations. New Eden was a stroke of genius on your part."

"We haven't got the girl yet."

"I trust you, Mo. So does the prophet."

"Moseby's here. I thought I was in charge."

"He's there as backup only. The prophet made that clear to him."

"Is that right?" Traveler said, relaying the comment to Moseby.

The First Apostle confirmed the fact.

"You see," Tanner said, "I take care of you when it counts."

"You mean I'm the fall guy if something goes wrong."

"God is with you now. I know it. The prophet has taken a turn for the better. The doctors say he's going to recover fully."

"Does Moseby know that?"

"That's why he volunteered to join you there and help, so I could stay behind and transmit the prophet's personal instructions."

"Willis says we're in charge," Traveler told his father.

The grimace on Martin's face said he was as leery of the setup as his son was.

"Go on," Traveler said into the phone.

"The prophet wants you to know how special Lael is to him."

"I understand."

"Do you? I don't think so."

"Out with it, Willis."

For a moment the only sound on the line was Tanner's heavy breathing. Finally he said, "I'm with the prophet right now, Moroni. In the same room. He'd speak to you personally, only the doctors don't want him tiring himself. Do you understand what I'm saying?"

"Willis, your men are wandering around in the dark out here. It will be a miracle if Kirkland doesn't hear us coming."

"Exactly, Moroni. A miracle is what we're talking about. The prophet says that one day Lael may become the church's first female apostle. But that can happen only if his long-range vision comes to pass."

Traveler shook his head at Martin. "Spell it out, Willis. Are we talking revelation?"

In the background he heard Elton Woolley's ragged voice. "Do anything you have to, Moroni, but save her for me. If you do . . ." His voice broke.

Traveler wet his lips. "Are you there, Willis?"

"I'm here."

"Tell the prophet I'll do my best."

"He knows that already."

"One more thing. I want Bill and Charlie out of jail."

"Consider it done," Tanner said.

35

The Danites, or whoever they were, had taken up positions about twenty yards back from the cabin, just beyond the edge of light cast by a pair of yellow porch bulbs. Even so, Traveler could make out their firing positions in the moonlight.

"Let's hope they haven't heard us moving in," Martin whispered.

"My men know what they're doing," Moseby responded.

"That's what I'm afraid of," Traveler said.

The three of them were crouched a few feet behind the perimeter, facing the cabin's front door. Pale shades had been drawn at the two flanking windows. Reuben Kirkland's camper, complete with the license plate once attributed to the Sisters Cumorah, was parked in an attached carport.

"Keep one thing in mind," Moseby said. "You don't want me for an enemy."

"Do your men know who's in that motel room?" Traveler asked.

Moseby whistled softly. The team leader crept over to join them.

"Tell him whatever you want," Moseby said.

Moseby sounded too sure of himself to trust, but Traveler wanted everything on the record. "Elton Woolley's niece is being held in that cabin."

"Yes, sir. I understand that."

"Her safety comes first."

"Yes, sir."

"Talk's fine," Moseby said, "but how do we get her out of there?"

If the Danites hadn't been present, Traveler might have suggested negotiation. Pick up the phone, explain the situation, and ask the kidnappers to surrender themselves and their hostage. But with so much firepower and so many zealous trigger fingers, he thought it best to control the situation himself.

"There's only one thing to do. I'm going in there." Traveler stood, pulling his father up with him.

After a moment, Moseby rose too. "If they take you hostage, Traveler, we'll be moving in."

"I want the sheriff in on this," Traveler said.

"Suit yourself." Moseby whistled again, a different signal than before. A moment later, the team leader arrived with Sheriff Hansen in tow.

"I'm going inside to try making a deal for the prophet's niece," Traveler told the sheriff. "If something happens to me, I expect you to protect her interests."

"I'll do my best."

"What about me?" Martin said.

Traveler reached out as if to shake hands. When his father took hold, Traveler pulled him into a bear hug and slipped him the .45.

"You protect *my* interests," Traveler whispered.

"Jesus. Both of us may have to be raised before this night's over."

"Remember," Moseby said. "You save the girl, but the kidnappers belong to us."

"I'm beginning to think you really are Danites."

Moseby chuckled softly. "That's nothing but old wives' tales."

The sheriff caught his breath before creeping away into the darkness.

"There goes your backup," Moseby said.

"Stay close to the First Apostle," Traveler told his father.

"Count on it."

Traveler moved forward into the yellow light, laced his fingers behind his neck, and stepped up onto the cabin's wooden porch. He tapped the door with his toe. The lights inside went out, but the porch bulbs stayed on. He heard movement a moment before the door opened a crack.

A man's voice said, "Let me see your hands."

Traveler unlaced his fingers and wiggled them near his ears.

"Are you alone?"

"Of course he's not alone," another voice said from inside the cabin.

"I don't see anybody."

"For Christ's sake, Wayne."

"Is that Wayne Farley and Reuben Kirkland?" Traveler said, remembering advice he'd gotten at the Cache & Carry Cafe in Paradise. Find one, you'll find the other. "I represent the prophet."

"That's us."

"Jesus, Wayne. Get him in here."

The door opened far enough for the porch light to glint on the barrel of a shotgun. Moving slowly, Traveler eased sideways across the threshold.

The door closed behind him an instant before the gun barrel jabbed him in the back.

"It's about time you got here."

"Think about it, Wayne," Kirkland said. "We haven't made the deal or set up delivery yet. Nobody should know we're here."

"Goddamn it, Roo. You said we were going to be rich."

"I did, didn't I." Kirkland snorted.

A small table lamp came on, its light as dingy as its parchment shade.

Traveler found himself staring into Lael Woolley's dark, yearning eyes. Her hands were tied to the arms of a chair, though her feet were free. A strip of silver duct tape covered her mouth.

Reuben Kirkland matched the description Traveler had been given, good-looking and blond with a California tan. The stainless steel revolver in his hand was a .357 magnum.

"Search him, Wayne."

Wayne Farley was dark-haired and wiry, with that ground-in dirt look that Utah's Carbon County coal miners get after too much digging. His blue steel shotgun was a pump model just like the sheriff's. He kept it in one hand while patting down Traveler with the other.

"Who the fuck are you?" Farley said when he finished his search.

Traveler smiled at the girl. "My name is Moroni Traveler."

"Sure," Kirkland said. "Give me your wallet." He checked the money before the ID. "What we've got here, Wayne, is a private investigator with thirty-two dollars to his name."

"Shit."

Traveler crouched in front of the girl. "Your uncle sent me."

Her face crinkled as if she were trying to speak behind the tape. She looked thinner than her photos and older, with dark patches under her red-rimmed eyes.

"Let me untie her?" he said.

Kirkland shook his head. "There's no way you came here alone."

"The First Apostle's outside with a platoon of Danites armed with automatic rifles."

"He's bluffing," Farley said.

Kirkland shook his head. "If they start shooting, she dies."

Traveler rose to his feet. "They know that."

Kirkland stepped around him and pressed the .357 against his neck. "Kill the light, Wayne, and take a look-see through the window."

"I always get the short end," Farley muttered, but did as he was told, being very careful with the window shade. "Nothing, for Christ's sake. Like I said, the guy's shitting us."

"Quiet. Let's listen. . . ."

Traveler kept himself perfectly still. After a while, Farley moved to the door and opened it just wide enough to accommodate his ear. The .357 trembled against Traveler's skin.

Half a minute passed before Farley closed the door and threw the deadbolt. "I told you. The guy's lying."

As soon as the light came back on, Kirkland faced Traveler again. "How'd you find us?"

"Let me get the tape off her," Traveler said, staring into the girl's pleading eyes.

Kirkland shrugged and moved back against the wall. "Suit yourself, but she was driving us crazy. We had to shut her up."

Traveler knelt down and gently peeled off the tape.

"God has sent the Angel Moroni to save me," Lael said the moment her lips came free.

"See what I mean? All she does is pray and fast. 'God's angel will come. God's angel will save me.' We've been hearing that for damn near a week. Only you don't look like an angel to me, or a Saint either."

"When the devil rises," Lael said, "God sends down an angel to fight him."

"Goddammit," Farley said. "Put the tape back on."

Traveler touched her cheek, a signal for silence. Her skin felt hot.

"I think she's got a fever," he said.

She smiled. "The fire of the Lord is with me now that you're here."

"Keep her quiet," Kirkland said, "and tell me how you found us."

"You told someone you were coming here."

"The hell I did."

"Several people mentioned paradise to me. I put two and two together. Paradise and Eden."

"I was born and raised here, but that doesn't make me crazy enough to tell anyone about it."

Traveler shrugged. "I got here though, with somebody's help."

"If you work for the prophet," Kirkland said, "what about our ransom?"

"A man like Woolley would never destroy his church to save his niece, or even his own life. You ought to know that."

"What the fuck are you talking about?" Farley, who had his back to the shaded window, emphasized his question with a wave of his shotgun.

"You can't kill an angel." Lael lurched to her feet, taking the chair with her.

The shotgun went off with a deafening explosion. Lael screamed and fell against Traveler, who hugged her to him as he dropped to the floor.

The shot triggered massive counterfire. The cabin shook. Glass shattered. The table lamp disintegrated.

Traveler cradled the woman against him, groping for the ropes that bound her. His hands grew wet, but he ignored what had to be blood and untied her.

Gradually, the shooting slacked off, then ceased altogether. A flashlight snapped on. Its beam found Wayne Farley, cut to pieces.

Kirkland redirected the light and exposed Traveler holding Lael. Her right shoulder and arm had taken most of the buckshot. One pellet had ripped open her cheek, narrowly missing an eye. There was a lot of seeping blood, but no arterial spurting.

She smiled up at Traveler. "Moroni's touch will heal me."

"I should have known better," Kirkland said. "Now get over to the door and call off your friends."

Friends would never have opened fire, Traveler thought as he made the journey on hands and knees, feeling for broken glass along the way. Direct hits had shattered the door in several places, but its mechanism still worked.

"This is Traveler," he shouted through a narrow opening. "Hold your fire. The girl's still alive."

"The next time someone makes a mistake and fires," Traveler heard his father say, "I'm going to shoot the First Apostle."

Traveler closed the door and crept back to Lael.

"I saw you in my dreams," she said.

"We thought she was hallucinating," Kirkland said, "because of all that fasting." He turned the light on Farley's dead face. "Look at Wayne there. She said God's wrath would be terrible, that He would strike us down."

The flashlight beam snapped back to catch Lael smiling. "See. She knows I'm as good as dead, too."

"Put your gun down and we'll all walk outside together," Traveler told him.

"Who's really out there?" Kirkland asked.

"Like I said, the First Apostle for one, Elihu Moseby."

"No police."

"Not unless you count the local sheriff. The guys with guns are church security. Maybe Danites. I don't know for sure. At this moment, my father's looking out for my interests. He'll make certain we get out of here alive. You can stay behind the girl all the way."

" 'The armies of Moroni encircled them about,' " she said, " 'and they were struck with terror.' "

Kirkland waved the light back and forth across her face. "We should have dumped her when they wouldn't pay the ransom."

"Say that again?"

"The girl gave us a number to call. It was supposed to get us through to her uncle, the prophet, or someone who could speak for him. We got through all right. You know what they said? They said they wouldn't pay. We figured they were negotiating at first, you know, trying to buy time or trace the call. So we moved around and called back, using pay phones. Nothing changed. 'No money,' they said. 'That's final.' "

"They told me you wanted a revelation?"

Kirkland angled the flashlight so his face was caught in its glow. His eyes were on Lael. "We asked for a hundred thousand—nothing but spit when you think about the church's money, its ten percent tithe coming in like clockwork. So why the fuss buying us off?"

"What about giving women the priesthood?" Traveler said.

"Jesus. You sound as crazy as she does."

Traveler thought that over. "Who did you talk to on the phone?"

"He didn't say." Kirkland shined the light in Traveler's face.

Squinting, Traveler said, "What did he sound like?"

"That's easy. A deep voice. I had the feeling I'd heard it before."

"God sounds like that," Lael said.

"So does Elihu Moseby," Traveler added.

"Oh, no. He doesn't speak for God. My uncle does."

"But one day Moseby will," Traveler reminded her.

"Uncle Elton worries about him, you know. About the succession. I think that's one of the things that made him get sick."

"He's better now," Traveler said. "I spoke with him just before I came here."

She sighed. "I should have known. My Angel Moroni has seen to everything."

"I'm dead," Kirkland said. "I think I knew it the moment that voice told me no money would be paid."

Traveler shook his head. "If you let the girl go, she can tell them you want to surrender."

Kirkland crawled forward until he was close enough to take Lael's hand. His gun was within reach but still pointed at her, so Traveler made no move.

"You should have taken me the way I was," Kirkland said. "I would have loved you then."

She pulled out of his grasp. "We are commanded to do God's work, to go among the Gentiles and enlighten them."

"Take her and get out of here."

Traveler lifted Lael into his arms and stepped to the door. Kirkland switched off the flashlight and opened the door.

Without exposing himself, Traveler shouted, "Dad, I'm bringing the girl out."

"My son speaks for the prophet," Martin answered.

Traveler risked a quick peek outside. Car lights came on to reveal his father standing in front of the cabin. Next to him was Elihu Moseby. Judging from the way the First Apostle was holding himself, Martin had the .45 placed strategically.

"I'd like to believe," Kirkland said. "I'd like to think I was going to heaven."

He pushed Traveler outside. As soon as Traveler reached his father, the automatic weapons opened fire again.

36

When Traveler arrived at the LDS Hospital, an entire section had been cordoned off by church security. He wasn't admitted until Willis Tanner was called to escort him personally to Lael's room.

Outside the door Tanner stopped and put a finger to his lips. "She insists on seeing you, but keep your voice down. The prophet's resting in the adjoining room."

"How is she?"

"The wound wasn't as bad as it looked. She didn't even need a transfusion. She could go home tomorrow, though I think the prophet wants to keep her near him for a while."

Lael's room, complete with a picture window overlooking downtown Salt Lake, was large enough to have its own sitting area. Her bed was full-size, not the standard small hospital model.

She lay propped on a stack of pillows, smiling at Traveler. Her eyes looked as feverish as ever, though her fingers felt cool when she took his hand.

Tanner nodded toward a connecting door and mouthed, "The prophet," before leaving the room.

"Sit here beside me," Lael said without letting go of his hand.

He eased onto the bed.

"You must think I'm a fool," she said, "allowing myself to get involved with someone like Reuben Kirkland. I'm sure I sounded crazy to you there in New Eden, calling you an angel."

"I've been called a lot worse."

"Uncle Elton told me all about you. A man to be trusted, he said. He's in your debt, by the way. He said so himself."

"There are no debts to be collected."

Her fingers tightened their hold on him. "I told Uncle Elton what I saw in my vision."

Not knowing what to say, Traveler only nodded.

"I see what you're thinking. It's on your face. You think lack of food affected my mind. Or fear maybe." She shook her head. "The veil between the living and the dead, between God and His children is very thin. That veil can become transparent at any time. It did for me. I saw through it the moment you came into that cabin. I saw you for what you are."

"I'm a Gentile," he said.

"You're my angel."

Her eyes closed. Her hand relaxed as if she'd suddenly gone to sleep. He freed himself and tiptoed from the room.

Tanner was pacing outside, looking distraught. When he saw Traveler he waved the newspaper he was holding. "Look at this, Mo. A special edition just arrived."

A huge headline read, RANSOM REVELATION. Underneath it, smaller print proclaimed, KIDNAPPERS KILLED IN SHOOT-OUT, PROPHET'S GRANDNIECE RESCUED.

"Read it," Tanner said. "They know everything."

Traveler scanned the text, which included details of the ransom demand—a false revelation, not the hundred thousand dollars Kirkland had confessed to. The story also mentioned Lael's membership in the Army of Nauvoo, hinting strongly that feminists were behind the kidnapping. The Army

189

of Nauvoo, the newspaper reported, was the subject of an ongoing police investigation.

"I don't understand it," Tanner said. "I thought I had a lid on the story."

"Where's Moseby?"

"Don't box me in, Mo."

"I told you why Kirkland was killed, to hush up the real ransom."

"You don't have any proof."

"What does Lael say?"

"She wasn't present when Kirkland made the phone calls."

"Did you pass the information on to Elton Woolley like I asked?"

"He's taking it under advisement."

"I talked to Mad Bill before coming here."

"So?"

"Before Newel Ellsworth was killed, he talked to Bill about Moseby."

Tanner grabbed hold of Traveler's arm. After a moment's resistance, Traveler allowed himself to be pulled down the corridor until they were well away from the prophet's room.

"He saw Moseby kissing his daughter," Traveler said. "Newel didn't realize she was his daughter. He thought they were lovers and followed them in a cab. They drove out to Magna and set fire to the house the Sisters Cumorah had rented."

"With Ellsworth dead that's hearsay."

"Maybe they started worrying about fingerprints. Who knows. Whatever it was, it got Newel killed." Traveler poked a finger against Tanner's chest. "I would have known about this sooner if you hadn't put Bill and Charlie in jail."

Tanner's tic started up.

"Like I said before, where's Moseby?"

"I'm having him watched like you asked. Right now, he's at the Lion House."

37

Brigham Young's Lion House was two stories of adobe and stone, dominated by a series of ten steeply pitched gabled roofs that created twenty back-to-back dormers. Each dormer had once marked the bedroom of one of Brigham's wives.

Moseby's empty limousine was parked in front. Across the street, a less conspicuous sedan held two men, presumably Tanner's. Ignoring them, Traveler walked up the stone path. At the door, he paused to admire the sculptured lion above the lintel. The carving alluded to Brigham Young's nickname, "The Lion of the Lord."

Lights were on inside despite the late afternoon sunshine. The storm front had passed to the north, hurried along by a high-pressure area now centered over the Great Salt Lake.

Traveler took a deep breath of fresh air and knocked on the door. A smiling Elihu Moseby opened it a moment later. At the sight of Traveler, the apostle's smile disappeared.

"Have you seen my daughter?" he said.

Traveler shook his head.

"She left me and went back to her husband." Shrugging, he waved Traveler inside. "I thought she might have changed her mind and come back."

The main meeting room looked as if Brigham Young had just stepped out, leaving behind rough-hewn pioneer furniture, old daguerreotypes, and handmade rag rugs. Even Moseby's black broadcloth suit, the kind favored by the Lion of the Lord, made Traveler feel as if he'd gone back in time.

Moseby pinched his nostrils. "You can still smell the women in here."

Traveler smelled only furniture polish.

Moseby ran his hand over the top of an antique desk. "When I'm in this room, I always feel close to those who've come before me."

He moved to the head of a long narrow dining table, set with rustic china and silverware, and sat down. "Do you know what my daughter said to me? 'Father,' she said, 'my husband, Seth, can protect me better than you can. Seth is closer to the prophet after all, related by blood.' " Moseby pounded the table. "The man's a weakling. When I'm prophet—"

"I don't think you're next in line anymore."

"God has spoken to me. I've done His bidding."

Traveler settled at the opposite end of the table. "Too bad we didn't get to talk after the shoot-out. I would have told you that Reuben Kirkland recognized your tabernacle voice on the telephone."

"The man's dead, never to be raised."

As a precaution against the mad glint in Moseby's eyes, Traveler slipped the .45 from his pocket and cradled it against his thigh. "You made sure of that, didn't you?"

"Proof, Mr. Traveler. That's what you need. Witnesses to confront me."

"I should have guessed that it was an old-fashioned kidnapping for money, not theology."

"I was speaking for God. You, a Gentile, never had a chance. Your likes never do. 'Divert the Gentile with the license plate,' my revelation said. 'Then call the newspapers and bring the Gentile running back when he's too close to finding the girl.' "

"I suppose the women I ran into outside Paradise were doing God's work too."

"You'll never know how much I enjoyed running you around in circles, to Paradise and back. My daughters loved it too. You should have heard them laughing when they told me how they'd cut you down to size."

Moseby threw back his head and laughed. At the movement, Traveler's finger took up the trigger slack.

"My daughters have abandoned me now," Moseby went on. "They should have remembered all the years I've spent accumulating favors. Seven of the apostles owe me. That's more than enough votes when the time comes."

Traveler forced himself to relax, to breathe evenly, to ease his finger away from the trigger. "You still have to answer to Elton Woolley."

"He's lost his way and no longer follows the path of God."

"And you do?"

"I've heard His revelations. By speaking to me directly, He has chosen me as the true successor. It's Woolley who's the false prophet."

Moseby tilted his head to one side as though listening to further instructions. " 'Honor the old ways,' God says. 'Make no changes in My name.' "

Traveler brought the .45 up from his lap and steadied it on the table so that it was aiming at the center of Moseby's chest.

The apostle smiled. "I fear you not, Mr. Traveler. You are not the hand of God. You don't hear Him as I do. 'I say unto you, ye must watch and pray always lest ye enter into temptation; for Satan desireth to have you, that he may sift you as wheat.' Do you realize what Satan has been whispering into Woolley's ear? That women are equal, that we should welcome them into our priesthood. To that, I say—God says—never. For years the spawn of Satan has been softening up the other apostles. One after the other, I watched them succumb to the serpent's tongue. But then God stepped in. Elton Woolley fell ill. If he had not, his blasphemous revelation would already be with us."

Moseby lowered his head as if in prayer. "Thank you, Lord, for showing me the way."

Traveler caught his breath. The trigger slack had been taken up again without conscious thought on his part. In that instant, he realized how badly he wanted to kill Moseby. Any excuse would do. Sudden movement, a threatening gesture, anything that would make the shooting self-defense.

Moseby continued. " 'Spread the word that the devil has risen,' God told me. 'Write it on walls throughout Zion. Bring the evil one down.' "

"How did you arrange the kidnapping?"

"It was manna from heaven. 'Ignore their demand for money,' the Lord told me. 'Substitute Satan's revelation. If Woolley gives in to them, denounce him as the Antichrist. If he does nothing, the girl will be killed so that all women may be blamed.' As of now, the women's movement is dead in this state. The old rules stand. Man must obey God. Women must obey their husbands."

"God didn't kill Newel Ellsworth."

The First Apostle flicked his hand as if shooing away an insect.

Traveler twitched. Why the gun didn't go off he'd never know. Sweat stung his eyes. His breathing grew so loud it echoed inside his head.

"That man was a hobo, a derelict," Moseby said. "You should be happy that he finally had a chance to serve God. The shedding of his blood atoned for all his sins."

By force of will, Traveler stood up and slipped the gun back into his pocket. "You lose, Moseby. I don't have to prove any of this in a court of law. The prophet has already called an apostles' court to try you."

Traveler and his father didn't arrive at the office until noon the next day. By then, the celebration was well under way in the lobby. Half a dozen bottles of imported scotch and another half-dozen bottles of wine were lined up on the cigar counter. The eternal flame had been relit. Enough cigar smoke was rising from Barney Chester, Mad Bill, and Charlie to blacken the mural of Brigham Young on the ceiling. Bill's sandwich board stood nearby, its placard blank.

"Thank God you're here," Bill said. "We've been waiting for you to open the bottles."

Charlie nodded vigorously.

"He says we couldn't have lasted much longer," Bill translated.

"Who's paying for all this?" Martin asked, eyeing Chester.

"Don't look at me. Bill says the booze is a gift from the prophet."

Bill grinned. "Actually, it came addressed to Moroni Traveler and Son from Willis Tanner. But you know him. He never makes a move without consulting the prophet first."

"A toast," Barney said, applying a corkscrew to one of the wine bottles. "To Newel Ellsworth."

Charlie spread out plastic cups on the countertop. Before anyone could drink, "Onward Christian Soldiers" assaulted them from the elevator.

"Nephi Bates got himself a boom-box," Chester shouted. "He says the Tabernacle Choir will ward off demons."

Traveler raised his cup and drank. The others did the same.

"I'm expecting someone," he said during a lull in the music. "A woman. Send her up when she gets here."

"You already have someone waiting for you upstairs," Bill said.

"Who?"

The sandwich prophet waved at the array of bottles on the cigar counter. "Who else? Willis Tanner."

A smiling Tanner, his face tic-free, was sitting at Traveler's desk.

"Take a load off, you two." Tanner pointed to the client's chairs, one in front of each desk.

The thought crossed Traveler's mind that he ought to remove Tanner bodily. Instead, he sat.

"Jesus," Martin muttered and stepped behind his desk.

"The prophet was well enough to leave the hospital," Tanner announced. "Not an hour ago, he was presiding personally over an apostles' court across the street." He jerked a thumb over his shoulder to indicate the temple.

"Well?" Martin said.

"The rumor was true. That's official now. The devil did rise to walk the land. He took on the appearance of Elihu Moseby. He became Moseby. Now Lucifer has been cast back into the pit."

"Excommunication?" Martin asked.

Tanner nodded. "From this moment on, the demon must be shunned. Those who ignore the prohibition forfeit their salvation."

Tanner's satisfied grin reminded Traveler that such a decree was totally binding on the faithful. Even the closest members of Moseby's family would be lost to him forever.

"There are those who favored the old ways," Tanner said. "But the spilling of blood frees a sinner. Satan's chosen one doesn't get off that easily."

"I almost feel sorry for Moseby," Martin said.

Tanner shook his head. "From now on, there can be no further mention of his name."

"What about Seth Woolley and his wife?" Traveler asked.

"Theirs is to be a late-life mission. Two years in the Asian wilderness seeking forgiveness. It's your doing. 'We owe it all to our two Moronis.' So said the prophet himself. 'I honor them as God's instruments. We Saints are in their debt.' "

"I wish he'd put that in writing," Martin said.

"The prophet has only one regret—his niece, Lael. Her chance is gone. The prophet is in no position now to receive a revelation on women's rights."

"Are you telling us he was about to give women the priesthood before this happened?" Traveler said.

"With the news of the kidnapping out, any such revelation would be tainted." Tanner stood up to leave. "There's one more thing. The prophet would like his carte blanche back."

Traveler rose to his feet. "Friends should be honest with one another, shouldn't they?"

Tanner nodded.

"They should protect one another."

Another nod.

"Bill and Charlie are friends too," Traveler said. "Yet you had them arrested."

"I had no choice."

"I didn't either."

"Oh, God, Moroni, you didn't give it to them."

"They're downstairs waiting. They promised not to hold you up for too much."

Martin closed the office door on Tanner's fleeing figure. "One of these days I'm going to look up that boy's ancestry. What with all that hanky-panky going on in pioneer times, I'd hate to think he was related to us. Speaking of which, I've decided to leave our family tree alone. There's no telling what we might find if we start shaking the branches hard enough."

"I thought Jolene was writing up our family history."

Martin smiled sheepishly and returned to his desk. "I've discovered we're not compatible."

"Since when?"

"Since she started talking about a temple marriage to seal us together forever."

"Stop ducking the issue."

"Your memory goes when you get to be my age."

The door opened before Traveler had a chance to reply. Stacie Breen was five minutes late for the appointment she'd made on the phone last night.

The last time Traveler had seen her, she'd been wet and disheveled. Now she was wearing a tailored gray suit with matching high heels and purse. Her hair looked and smelled as if she'd just come from the beauty parlor.

Martin stood up while Traveler held the client's chair for her.

"Gentlemen," she said, "seeing you like this almost makes me sorry I sold my interest in Moroni Traveler and Son."

Traveler looked at Martin, who shook his head and sighed.

"I warned you I was going to hold an auction," she said, "for information received."

"How much did you get?" Traveler asked.

She stood up and slowly turned around to show off her clothes. "Enough for two weeks on the coast in style."

"I don't suppose you'd tell us where the boy is anyway," Martin said.

"My lips are sealed."

"Tell us the name of the buyer at least."

"That's why I'm here."

She stepped around the desk to the window, beckoning them to follow.

"Look down there," she said.

Traveler saw Mad Bill first. He was standing on the sidewalk in his sandwich board peering at the top floor of the Chester Building. His message, in letters large enough to read three stories up, was MORONI LIVES.

"So what?" Martin said.

"It's her," Traveler said, "Lael Woolley. She's standing next to Bill."

She, like Bill, was staring up at them.

Stacie waved.

Lael and Bill waved back.

"She owns you now," Stacie said. "Just like Claire."

As soon as Stacie left the office, Martin clapped his son on the back. "I can tell from here that girl's a true missionary at heart."

Martin raised the window and leaned out. Lael waved harder than ever.

"You're a lucky man," Martin said. "Not every woman knows a soul in need of saving when she sees one."